KERRY HADLEY-PRYCE was born in Wordsley, in the West Midlands, in 1960. She worked nights in a Wolverhampton petrol station before becoming a secondary school teacher. She wrote *The Black Country* whilst studying for an MA in Creative Writing at the Manchester Writing School at MMU, for which she gained a distinction and was awarded the Michael Schmidt Prize for outstanding achievement 2013–14. She lives in the Black Country.

THE BLACK COUNTRY

Kerry Hadley-Pryce

SALT

CROMER

PUBLISHED BY SALT

12 Norwich Road, Cromer, Norfolk NR27 0AX United Kingdom

Printed in Great Britain by Clays Ltd, St Ives plc

Typeset in Sabon 10/13

ISBN 978 1 78463 034 8 paperback

1 3 5 7 9 8 6 4 2

THE BLACK COUNTRY

L ET'S BE CLEAR about something from the off: small cats share the same instincts as large cats. The same impulses. I read that somewhere. And I'm sure of it now. Absolutely sure. It's depressing. And, before we start, it's lies that kill relationships, not affairs. That's important. And it's important that all these bits and pieces of lies are out in the open. It is. We need to be clear on this. And we just have to hope it's enough.

Maddie's bits and pieces were all over the floor. The upturned bedside table, the unmade bed, the memory of last night. There it all was. This is what Harry says. Picture it. Maddie Harper's bits and pieces of lies all over the floor.

'Maddie,' Harry would have said, hopeful she might be there somewhere.

He would have opened the curtains, Harry would, he would have seen that outside it had stopped snowing, but the sky sagged grey. To him, the street might have seemed dead. He would, most likely, have seen his footprints crunched into the snow; uneven marks approaching round the corner, past the neighbours' houses, past the lamp post, across the garden, right up to the door. But from his high angle he would certainly have been able to see another, smaller set of footprints leaving the house and, at the kerbside, where Maddie's car should have been, a shaded, snowless rectangle, and tyre marks where she'd driven away.

At first, he says he thought she'd left him, again. Says he couldn't help himself. This was always his first thought. His first fear. He says he tried to stop himself from reliving that moment fifteen or so years back when he'd come home and she wasn't there. She'd gone, left him. He's insecure, Harry Logue is. That's one of his problems. So, when he came home and her bits and pieces were all over the place, he says the thought crossed his mind that she might have found out about what he'd done, that she'd put two and two together. All that guilt. And what was going on in his head – all his thoughts, guilty thoughts, bouncing around his head like a fly against a light-bulb. All those thoughts mixing up and coming to the conclusion that she might have left him, again, like she did before.

But it wasn't about that, or Jonathan any more, this was about Harry, and he thought she'd gone.

And who could blame her really?

When he looked, though, he could see their suitcases were still balanced on top of the wardrobe and her shoes were still piled in the corner of the room. When he opened a drawer, he says it was still brimming with her underwear. He says he pulled out a pair of her knickers and felt the material – not silk but something like it – and brushed it against his lips, feeling it catch on winter-dried skin. He remembers reaching into his back pocket, getting his mobile phone out, calling her. She still has the message he left on her answerphone, his voice stringy, forced: 'Hi, Maddie, it's me. Where are you? Come home. I'm home now. We'll talk. I want to talk, I do. We can sort it all out. Come home. I'm here now. Just come home.'

He says he sat down on the bed – their bed – and the screen of his mobile phone faded to black in his hand.

And he would have sat and waited, praying, in his own way, that she would come back.

But Maddie was with me. Where else would she be?

Looking back on it all, we might wonder where the beginning is. The beginning of all of this. It might be difficult to see. But for Harry, it's a funeral. Gerald somebody. His funeral. And Harry might be right. This Gerald person did have a part to play in all this. If it wasn't for him, after all, they'd never have met.

So this funeral is the beginning for Harry. It's apt.

He says both he and Maddie had taken the afternoon off work to attend the service. She, probably anxious not to be late, worried about appearing too jovial. She might have just tied up the sale of a house she'd been working on for too long in the estate agency where she'd worked for a couple of years. She was probably careful to have removed her blue nail polish and red lipstick. He, unnerved by funerals, always anxious about saying the wrong thing, amazed he'd managed to get cover for his lessons at the secondary school he'd taught at for ever. Both, he says, arrived on time, but separately. She might have greeted him by straightening his tie (borrowed), he might have made a weak attempt to kiss her (failed, but no matter) and there, just right there, was a glimpse of a deepening sense of something – disappointment or something more – between them. Disappointment, that's what Harry says now.

According to Maddie, it rained. Great big drops. 'Wet rain' she calls it. Rain that blurs things. Rain that makes you run. So they say they ran. They ran into the little church and re-member sketchy details like the coffin looking too small for a man who'd spent his entire career in the English depart-ment at the University of Wolverhampton, where they'd both met him, studied for their degrees. They remember the vicar talking about how there'd never be another man like Gerald. A good man. A kind man. A man who, despite his twenty a day habit didn't deserve that horrible, protracted, painful death, or, probably, that small, cheap-looking coffin. No flowers. All donations to Cancer Research. Poor Gerald. And so on.

Old Gerald's widow, Ava or Eva or Vera, probably sat

without crying in that painfully, beautifully brave, washed-out way that new widows do. Next to her, according to Harry, a youngish man, a young Gerald – his son – wearing a pink tie, head uptilted, swallowing hard. He has a part to play in all this, if only he knew. And according to Maddie and Harry, there were very few others in that intensely cold church. And there they were, in the midst of death, watching their own breath.

We'll have to try to forgive the gaps in their memory. We must credit them with a depth of feeling for Gerald. Lovely Gerald who guided them both during their university years, who had mentored them through their dissertations, who kept them on track.

'Madeleine and Harry,' he had apparently said to them at their joint tutorials. 'You just need to apply yourselves. Keep up with your work, attend lectures, stop asking for extensions to assignments. Procrastination is what you seem to have in common. You should both just get on with it. Life's too short, don't mess it up.'

And Harry remembers Gerald lighting up another Rothman's and sending them on their way.

Procrastination. Old Gerald was right. Maddie's ideas had all been there, they had. But they were buried deep inside her, banging against the confused, directionless energy of her youth. And Harry, wanting to be all authority-intolerant, but usually exhausted with dread that he might have blinked and missed something, in the social sense only of course. Such a long time ago now, getting on for twenty years. And they thought they'd survived the procrastination, thought they'd applied themselves, got on with it.

So there they were, at this funeral, probably with blobs of faded mottled light rippling through orange and green stained glass; pictures of Mary and Jesus deflecting across their faces, not that they would have noticed, celebrating the life of the man who brought them together. Imagine it.

Harry pads out his memory of this day quite a bit. Maybe what he tells us is important. We'll decide that. He tells of a time during the service when he reached for Maddie's hand, prompted by what he calls a 'prickle of a memory' – Harry's the type to say things like that – a prickle of a memory of a time when Gerald suggested the two of them work together, help each other out, pool ideas. So they worked together for the first time, reading some book or other. Harry says he wasn't sure he got it, but Maddie did. Maddie got it, she understood it. If we let her, she'll go on about how she found it all so brilliant, and Harry, being Harry, sort of fell for her then. That's what he says. Fell for her as she was talking about this book he didn't understand. He'll recall the way the scene had played out all those years ago, the way Maddie yielded to him, the warmth of her, the smell of her, the simplicity and ease of it all, and so the prickle made him reach for her hand, in that church. It was a reaction to that sentimental memory. Typically, for Harry, he says he wanted to touch her right there, at that funeral, just some contact, some connection re-established. But just as he began to reach out, just as his hand shifted towards hers, just at that very second, he says Maddie sneezed. A quiet squeak of a sneeze, stifled well by covering her nose and mouth with both hands. Moment lost. Prickle gone. Maddie maintains she doesn't remember this, of course, and Harry, well, Harry's feelings are different.

Outside, he says, rain continued to fall. It fell on the coffin as it was lowered into the ground, it struck the yew trees and skittered off onto the moss below, it dripped down Gerald's son's face and it probably seemed to reduce everyone's life to blurry shapes; imprecise, hazy, diluted.

Maddie says she was relieved when it was over, the funeral

that is. She says she was soaked through, glad to be directed to the local pub where there were post-funeral sandwiches, and drinks. Had she been alone, she would certainly have ordered a large glass of red – very large. She would have. She would have drunk the first one quickly, got the taste. The second one she would have savoured for a little longer, but not until the third would she have sat in the corner and enjoyed the relaxation of it. That's Maddie.

'Having a drink?' Harry remembers asking.

Yes, if she had been alone, she would have followed those glasses of red with a large brandy. Maybe two.

'Orange juice. Thanks,' she said, but there was an edge to her voice and Harry says he caught it.

'You sure? You don't want something else?'

'No, just orange juice.'

A pause. It would have been one of those irritating ones, like a cat about to pounce.

'Sure? I mean I don't mind if you want a drink. I'll drive, we can leave your car here.'

'Oh, for God's sake Harry. Just a bloody orange juice.' Maddie would have tried to keep her voice low. 'That's what I asked for.'

Now, if we'd have been there, if we could have listened carefully, we would have heard the creak and groan of the foundations of their life. Harry heard it – he says he did – but he says he bought her the bloody orange juice without another word and watched her drink it. Every mouthful. And every swallow will have looked sour, toxic. If we suppose he was enjoying her discomfort, we'd be wrong. Fact was he was looking at her but he says he was noticing how her hair hung like damp cardboard that day, framing a square jaw, very white skin. To him, something seemed to have withered her a little, she seemed smaller, scooped-out somehow. She had been the girl who'd

6

cycled everywhere to meet him, who'd sung rugby songs to amuse him, who'd once written a short story for *Pulp Erotica* and had read it aloud to him. What had happened to her? This is what Harry was thinking.

'What are you looking at?' she apparently said, after a moment or two.

'Nothing,' he said.

It's not that Harry is a complete fool. Not at all. Every day, he says he makes an attempt to take hold of his life, even though it's not the life he planned. He'll tell us that most of the anxieties he felt as an undergraduate have gone. He'll try to convince us he's developed a calmer approach to life, so, rather than grabbing the rhythm of the day and dancing with it, in reality, he usually just avoids facing the music, tries to avoid worrying about what seems to be the hyper-reality of his life: the rude students in the bottom set groups, the constant pressure, the worry of making each day, each child, matter. Being a teacher, he says, has taught him patience, tolerance, anxiety management. He says his father, a GP, always said, 'Take three paracetamol to lift depression.' And some mornings – most mornings – he does just that. Even now, after all that has happened, he says he'll try to get better. Try to be a better person.

Don't be fooled by him though. He, like us, finds ways with which to release his various tensions. He does.

When Maddie looks back at the day of Gerald's funeral, she'll remember most clearly the pub, its smells and sounds of wine and men. She'll remember the imprint of working men still visible in every speck of grime in that pub. She'd been there before, in this place, without Harry, many times. She says she thought the barman recognised her but she didn't acknowledge him, feigning ignorance – something she's good at. She says she felt a sudden twinge of something and might have said something like, 'Why do I always forget my umbrella?' and surprised herself with her own inanity.

Harry's eyebrows apparently shot up into a furrow and she says she knew he was delaying swallowing a mouthful of shandy.

'My umbrella would have been useful today.' Her voice would have trailed off and she probably drained her orange juice in one go.

Harry would have swallowed and said nothing.

To an outsider, they were, are, an odd-looking couple. Harry with his awkward stance, looking uncomfortable, out of place or out of time somehow. Some women, girls, apparently, think he could be attractive, handsome even, if he just made an effort. If he wore different clothes, got a decent haircut, bulked up a little. Some girls think all that could make a difference. They do. And leaning against the bar of that pub, he probably looked a little shy, younger than his years, smooth-faced, maybe a little shifty – the man who was the boy who had sand kicked in his face – somehow bereft. Several times, he says he tried to catch someone's eye, anyone really, and each time they ignored him. It's because he seems to have very little presence. It's like he isn't sure of anything at all. Odd for a teacher really. To look at him, you'd think he was an accounts clerk or a storeman of some kind. His fingers are longish, his hands clean, soft – as if he might use hand-cream or hand-gel. He holds a pint glass, but the drink's mainly lemonade, a kid's drink. Next to him, we can imagine Maddie, empty glass in hand. On first glance looking every bit the English Rose, but if you look again you'll notice there's a sort of relaxed energy about her features, a defensive strength in her posture that makes it difficult to guess her age. She could be fifteen or fifty, or anywhere in between. If you were a woman, you might wonder where the hell she got that dress – it looks too big, too long, too old-fashioned – it covers too much of her. Figures like hers are the ones women generally crave. Outsiders might ask what do they see in one another? Why are they even together, these two?

And there's something else. It's difficult to explain, but it's as if a sort of seventh veil settled between them some time ago. And it would have been visible, right there as they sat, or stood or whatever, looking in opposite directions. It would have been as if everything that had gone before had silently smothered them, like a fragile membrane. No matter what they say, they didn't realise that completely then. They just didn't.

They say they received the invitation the next day, by phone. Maddie had just left for work. Another day of drudgery and pointless cajoling at the office. Probably late, looking tired, but showing other symptoms that morning, maybe a little peaky-looking. Pinched, maybe. Still, she says she had managed a mouthful of tea, fluttered a dishcloth across the work surfaces and as the telephone rang, was most likely crunching into second gear and cursing the clutch. The message on the answer machine, the message that remains there still undeleted, was from a voice sounding chipper for so early in the morning:

'Ah, thought I might catch you before work. Not to worry, just wanted to thank you for coming to Dad's funeral. Lovely to see you both, just sorry you had to leave so early. Wanted to invite you to a reunion really. Thought it might be good to get some of dad's old graduates together, you know . . . Don't know if you'll be interested? Well, give me a call if you are. I know dad would have liked it.' Something like that.

They have replayed this message a hundred times since, Maddie and Harry have. They say they have, anyway.

And that day, it was pretty standard for both of them, so they say: Harry, at work with his ham-fisted attempts at educating today's youth in Shakespeare and semi-colons. Maddie, shivering in her cardy, cursing each infrequent punter who dared to enter the dreary estate agency. Both of them most likely loathing their shop-bought sandwiches, both stomaching a different brand of cheap, instant coffee and both willing the day to end. At some point in the day, it had occurred to both of them that this was no way to live, and both of them had asked themselves how they had managed to reach this point, this low point. The thoughts weren't simultaneous of course – Harry says his occurred just after mid-morning break and the unusual arrival of the Principal into his classroom.

'Not staying,' the Principal apparently said, in amongst a troupe of girls arriving early for the lesson. 'Just need you to drop in and see me. Tomorrow before school. 8ish?'

Harry nodded but says he felt his heart battle to keep control. An unscheduled, uncalendared meeting like this was not good. Normally, of course, provided you've been doing your job, provided you've nothing to hide, there should be nothing to worry about. Harry had been doing his job as best he could, but that's not necessarily saying much.

And, fact is, we all have something to hide.

And there it was. The thought in Harry's head: how did we get to this point?

Maddie would have arrived at this question later on in the day. She says one of her sales fell through. In other months, Maddie would have sworn a little, smoked a sneaky cigarette, maybe, and made sure she sold the property to someone else by the time she went home. That day, however, she says she was sick. Physically sick. She received the call from an apologetic vendor, and then, right there, just in time to get to the poky staff toilet, Maddie says she was sick.

And that was when she would have thought: We can't live like this. We absolutely can't.

Harry says he came straight home from work that day. He would have been pre-occupied and that's why he would have missed the red flash of the answer machine, even in the gloom of their hallway. Instead, he would have headed for his computer. We can try to imagine it. And even those who think they know him well would have thought he cut a peculiar figure that day, lurching in as he would have, seemingly unaware of the earthy cold in their house. Most would have expected him to flick on the central heating, curse himself for not having sorted the timer out, maybe boil the kettle, but Harry says he didn't do any of that. So, it was Maddie who, having so nearly taken the call that morning, caught the urgency of the flashing light, pushed 'play' and took the message.

When they look back, when they re-run the scene, try to lay the blame, even they find it difficult.

Recalling that time, that early evening, Maddie says she remembers odd things like the sibilance of the voice on the answer machine and the way it cut through a sort of mustiness that seemed to have been threatening to settle for months, years. She remembers Harry in the kitchen, not at his computer. She remembers a conversation. Something like:

'Can you smell damp?' Maddie, asking.

'Was that Gerald's son on the phone?' Harry now.

'I can smell damp, or something, can't you?'

'What's that he said about a reunion?'

'So hungry.'

'Shall I call him back?'

'Have we got any food?'

'I'll call him back.'

Looking back, we can try to imagine Maddie's head hunched, obscured as she foraged in the fridge. Knowing Maddie, all there would have been was microwaveable lasagne, a pack of out-of-date leeks or the crusty edge of month-old cheddar. Not good. She's not a good housekeeper is Maddie. But that sickness from earlier had left her feeling empty and nauseous with hunger. What she wanted was something vinegary. Pickles, yes. Beetroot. That's what she says. We might imagine her starting to get desperate. Desperate with hunger or whatever. Meantime, in the hall, to her, Harry would have been just a hazy silhouette on the telephone. His conversation with Gerald's son? Functional, probably. A list of mental tick-boxes quickly ticked off, where and when the reunion was to be held, and a swift, polite acceptance. When he returned to the kitchen, he says Maddie was heating soup on the stove. To Harry, watching her standing there, it seemed as if she had used up her entire supply of energy, of life, really. Harry says he spoke first.

'I talked to him. It's on Saturday out at Oakhall Manor. A reunion.'

Maddie should have replied, should have found some response. She should have said something, she says she didn't really want to go, but instead, she says she just stirred the soup and nodded. Harry should have grown restless, irritated. Maybe he wanted to, but there was much on his mind, quite a tangle of complexities there. In his own words, 'there wasn't much cognitive surplus left for spontaneity.'

Pathetic. Both of them.

So, they would have eaten the soup. She, concentrating, probably swallowing as much as she could as quickly as she could, scraping the spoon across and around the dish, leaving sticky brown-white lines where she refused to leave a single drop, clinking the spoon inside the dish when she'd finished. He, floundering after the second mouthful, and with a vague gesture of resignation and a pained expression, giving up. Maddie would have hesitated. For a moment she might have looked as if she'd ask him what was wrong. There is a precise second when she says she looked right at him, and sensing a meaning in his eyes, sat motionless, suspended somewhere in time. But she says a whirl of nauseous hunger seemed to over-power her and the only thing she could do was reach for his unfinished soup and say something like, 'Don't throw it away, I'll finish it.'

It's very easy to be evil. Even by accident. Accidental evil. I read somewhere about someone, some judge or other, who said something about society containing naughty girls doing grown-up things and then bitterly regretting them.

Depends on our viewpoint. As to whether we regret any-thing, is what I mean. It's a lovely idea, regret is. Probably best to keep it all locked up, not expose it to the light of day.

Regret, that is, not evil.

Maddie says she awoke slowly the next morning. Spasms of winter rain had bothered the silence in the room, and, eyes still shut, she says she rolled over outstretching her arm into an empty space. She must have slowly realised she forgot to set the alarm. She says she felt she was beginning to forget things. She most likely got up out of bed carefully, and, with that sort of dark lethargy she has, stood up, opened the cur-tains and looked outside. It was still dark, so she says. That awkward kind of Black Country darkness, probably, and she says she shivered as if she'd suddenly fallen into freezing wa-ter, or someone had walked over her grave. She says she knew she needed to get a grip on the day, take a shower. So she did. But, poor Maddie, the smell of the shampoo, the feel of the water, they pierced something in her, and before she knew it, she says there was that nausea again. And nothing could rid her of it. Nothing. No amount of retching, no amount of sweating or swallowing or hyperconcentration on mind over matter. And as she sat gracelessly on the floor in the corner of the bathroom, she says she trembled as she wept. And later whilst Maddie dressed – all black that day, she says – Harry probably waited outside the Principal's office, pretending he didn't care, most likely attempting banter with a group of sixth formers arriving early, probably ignoring the enquiring glances of those he called 'colleagues'. Harry's keen to tell us it was 8.10 am when the Principal appeared from the far end of the quad. From Harry's viewpoint, he – this Principal – is a crow-like man, stiff and tall, presiding over them all with a nasty superiority, in a black suit, driving a black car. They call him the Undertaker and, according to Harry, he just seems to be waiting to snap your coffin closed and bury it whether you are alive or dead. Harry says he suspected there was a coffin waiting for him inside the Principal's office, and in a way he was right. The crows were circling overhead.

He should have found it worrying that day, surely. He should have felt a little worried. This was his career, wasn't it? He should have heard the caw-caw from a distance, felt at the very least sad. But he didn't. He says he didn't. In fact, as the Principal approached him, it's possible that Harry felt a jab of something like joy in his heart. Unaware of the rain vexing the grass on the playing field and leaking in through the roof, or of Maddie's tears back in their bathroom for that matter, Harry says he stepped into the Principal's peculiar, windowless office and closed the door.

Harry speaks freely about this meeting, that heart-cracking time in that nasty office: the opening of the filing cabinet, the pulling out of the file, the grave glance at the wristwatch, the vague smell of disinfectant. And the conversation beginning 'Now, Mr Logue . . .' And then a horrible pause. Really, with hindsight, Harry knows he should have spoken up at that point. He should have steered the conversation in a way that placed him more in charge, in control. He should have prepared a defence. But, as usual, he was too slow. So when the Principal said, 'I've been meaning to have a word with you for a while now,' Harry's admits his response was idiotic and stammering.

'I know . . .' he said, 'I sort of hoped you would . . . but . . .'

'The thing is,' the Principal was ignoring him, 'we have a problem.'

Another of those pauses.

A pause and a flick through the file. Imagine it now.

Harry says his mind seemed to go completely blank, says it drained out quite suddenly. This is how he remembers it. No joy, no fear, just nothing, and it will have shown on his face. Like a man facing a firing squad the moment before they cover his eyes.

'I need you to be honest, Harry.'

Honest. Harry says the word stung the air.

I will, Harry thought, I will, I'll explain. Let me explain.

'Just tell me if I've got it wrong.' The Principal apparently leaned forward, hands clasped as if in prayer. 'But something has been brought to my attention about you.'

Harry's paralysis can't have been noticed by the Principal. Perhaps we only see what we expect to see, and anyway, Harry says the file-flicking had begun again.

'Morals and ethics.' The Undertaker was caw-cawing now. 'What's your take?'

'My take?' Harry said, eventually. We can guess he was visibly thrown a little, actually trying to formulate a confession of sorts. Harry says his 'take' was that he was about to be tortured, made to suffer, that the bastard was going to enjoy making him squirm. And he says he felt momentarily affronted.

'Morals and ethics?'

'Yes, well, Moral Philosophy really. All that *Beyond Good and Evil* stuff. Nietzsche, is it?'

We can imagine that Harry was lost now, but he says he remembers the sound of a girl, hooting with laughter outside in the corridor, in that inexplicable way teenage girls do, and for a split second both men's attention was drawn to the door, probably thinking she was going to burst in. Maybe prompted by the sudden jab of time and reality, the Principal said, 'Your degree. I notice it contains some Philosophy. Do you think you could teach some in upper school? Margaret's just announced she's pregnant, again, and I can't see another way round it. No-one else has a clue. I really don't want to advertise, haven't the time, do you think you could do it justice? Be honest.'

Not even Harry would have guessed this conversation, this brief meeting would have gone on to contain the words 'advancement' and 'promotion' and 'increased salary'.

Imagine him, Harry, sitting there in that office, grappling with the prospect of accepting a temporary promotion to a post he didn't want in a job he loathed and wasn't much good at. Imagine that. Imagine how appalled he must have felt at the trust, the faith, the desperation of it all.

Of course he accepted it. What else would he do? He was an easy target. But then Harry was always that.

Leaving the Principal's office, Harry says he looked out across the corridors, out across the quad and the playing fields beyond. It had stopped raining, but the roof above him probably continued to leak. And Maddie, back at home, she was still crying.

Did they celebrate, Maddie and Harry? Did they celebrate Harry's promotion with champagne or dinner out somewhere nice, or a cosy little glass of something? Did they plan how they might save or spend the extra cash? Did they have an early night, make love like they used to, thinking only of the future, of themselves in the future and how lucky, lucky, lucky they were?

Not a chance.

Maybe it would have been different if Harry had mentioned anything, if he'd actually told her about his day. But he didn't. And anyway, he was late, so he says, and when he arrived home she was in bed half asleep. His late arrival would have meant nothing to her. She says she hardly noticed except for the tug of the duvet as he crept into the chilly space beside her.

And they lay there, both of them mostly awake with their eyes closed, doubtless both of them with their various insecurities working away in their heads. Both of them, at that stage unaware of what the future held.

Even today, if we ask them, if we were able to ask them, their story might change, waver just a little.

With some certainty, both Maddie and Harry will describe the humdrum mechanics of getting ready for the reunion, the one organised by Gerald's son. It was a Saturday, that's true. It's not particularly important, but Maddie recalls agonising over what to wear. Dress or trousers? Dark or bright colours? Harry remembers her wearing a dress, dark red, maroon. He remembers the beginnings of an argument before they left, something about his untidy computer desk, but he's evasive or can't remember much about it. And then the journey: uneventful. Maddie was determined to drive because the act of driving relieved her of the responsibility of conversation. Besides, in truth, she wanted to take her car so that she would have a reason not to drink. Trying to be good, so she says. Harry didn't argue, and his memory seems equally clear about that, and it's important. Maddie drove.

The road to Oakhall Manor eventually thins out to a winding lane for a mile or so before a single-track drive to the car park. Locals ironically call this stretch The Straits and it makes arrival at Oakhall slightly more memorable. That night,

Maddie, concentrating on silence, would have missed the sight of the blue and orange and purple night collapsing behind her as she headed out from the gritty Midlands towards the intermittent promise of the Worcestershire hills. It might just have been the time of year, but Maddie remembers the trees lining this road seemed to crowd in towards her. Everybody says this. It's an illusion of course, but there's an impression that in passing through, in leaving behind that toxic-looking Black Country landscape, you're disloyal somehow, that in leaving the town you have broken a promise, that you've forsaken something. It could just have been the winter dark. That, maybe, and the hungover air from industrial estates. That night Maddie remembers seeing lightning forking, yellowish across the hills ahead of her. But she continued to drive, silently concentrating, and Harry, she remembers him as impassive, silently thinking beside her.

Yes, it would be good, more entertaining to report some kind of conversation, but there was none, apparently. No music either. No radio. Only a brittle whirr of machinery – the engine, a blast from the heater, the various scales of sound as both Maddie and Harry would have drifted away from each other.

So. There's a steep, narrow slope of a lane before you reach the raw commercial interruption that is Oakhall Manor. Is it mock Tudor? It's the sort of place that's a venue for second marriages or weekends away, or office Christmas lunches. It's not that far from the rough end of town, but the fact of having to arrive via a drive flanked by darkness and clipped hawthorn hedges can fool you into thinking you've escaped. You haven't of course. And that night, the night of the reunion, Maddie and Harry were under no illusions. In fact, as they arrived, they both felt the same way, so they say, not really looking forward to it, uncomfortable, aware of the necessity to play out their parts like actors in a film. Only duty made them attend. Gerald would probably have liked it.

As they got out of the car, both say they were immediately aware of the smell of cold water, faintly bitter. Somewhere nearby there was a brook or a spring, or a leaking pipe, or something and the prickly moist air made them sharpen their stride across the tarmac. When they think back to this moment, the moment they rushed into the warmth, the moment they saw Jonathan Cotard, isn't it interesting that both Maddie and Harry use the same word to describe it? At first, both of them say it seemed 'uneventful'. They're trivialising, minimising the situation. And at first, when they recall that meeting, they agree with each other that they saw Jonathan Cotard that Saturday. They agree a couple of other things: that they spoke about Gerald, the weather, their jobs. Small talk. And they talk about Jonathan as if this was the very first time they'd ever met him. They say they were both surprised at how comfortable they felt in his company. Jonathan, they say, had been one of Gerald's first batch of students, not their cohort, a little older. Nice chap. This is what they'll tell us, at first.

According to Harry, though, there were only a few people there when they arrived. Some they recognised, most they didn't. He says the room felt warm, cosy, and there was that commercial smell of coffee and beer and food and firewood, which eased him. The barman smiled at them and Harry says he approached him as manfully as he could, feeling his shoes slick across the thick carpet, and says he began to think maybe the evening wouldn't be too bad after all. And it was whilst Harry ordered drinks that Maddie would have wandered away. Minutes later, Harry says he caught sight of her talking to a man. He watched as they spoke, voyeur that he is, and he remembers she looked 'ripe'. That's the word he used. When pressed, Harry says she had a wild look about her.

Self-assured. Her hair looked longer, glossier. Her skin, paler. And her lips, Harry says it was like he'd never noticed her lips before. Even now, he can't really explain what he means – he says he can't explain. He says it might have been something to do with the light or maybe about the way she tilted her head, the way she looked at that man – Jonathan – the way that red dress clung to her body. The maroon of it. And her body – nothing particularly obvious – certainly not flirty, not really, not to him, but he says there was a peculiar, overfilled flexibility about her, an animation that gave her a kind of ripeness. And Harry remembers he felt a sudden grief, so thick and deep and long, he says it might have been love, or something. He says he watched her for a second or two, noticed the way she angled her face, the way she pushed her hair away from her forehead, the way her eyes looked greener somehow, even from a distance. Next to that man she looked strangely young, looking up, enraptured, or so it seemed, by something he was saying.

'Harry.' A voice beside him. Gerald's son, saying something about being pleased to see them, something like that. Harry says he was looking over to where Maddie was.

'Ah, she's with Jonathan.' Harry remembers Gerald's son leaning in, and leading Harry over to them, Maddie and Jonathan, standing close.

Harry says it was odd but he remembers feeling embarrassed, like an intrusion, a pathetic interruption. The drinks he was carrying slopped over his fingers. He says he felt foolish.

'Jonathan,' Gerald's son said. 'Let me introduce Harry Logue to you. You've already met the lovely Madeleine by the looks of things. Maddie, you look absolutely lovely. Thank you for coming.'

There would have been an exchange of a quick kiss between Maddie and Gerald's son – Maddie and her kisses, it's inevitable – and a handshake between Harry and Jonathan. Harry's sticky, loose handshake.

Maddie took the drink without looking and Harry says he traced her look to Jonathan's face. Up close, he says Jonathan seemed taller, easily more than six feet tall. Neither young nor old, one of those men whose age was impossible to guess, but he was certainly old enough to be a man with a purposeful grip on life. This was true. He looked at Harry with grey eyes and a comfortable smile. And a nod.

'Jonathan was Dad's first success,' Gerald's son said.

They both remember Jonathan adjusting his gaze, and there was a pause. Harry says he, Jonathan, held a glass of something that looked like whisky. And just beneath the cuff of his shirt, the bracelet of a watch was visible, glinting gold. If Harry had known much about watches, he'd have known then that it was a Patek Phillipe original, but what he says he noticed were Jonathan's long fingers – pianist's fingers, or artist's fingers maybe – and his slim wrist and oddly milky skin. He says he noticed how little black hairs had invaded the back of Jonathan's hand. And then the cut of his trousers, good quality, the way the material fell against his legs. This is what Harry will tell you.

'Well, that was when I was young.' Harry remembers Jonathan speaking slowly, the intonation of another local town. Harry says he couldn't quite place it.

'Gerald's successes,' Harry said. 'Yes, well, can't say I count myself among them.'

It was meant to be self-deprecating, and it is a tactic Harry often uses. Too often for Maddie's liking, and it would have shown on her face. A micro expression of agitation, a slightly slower blink, a very light sigh. Jonathan would have noticed it.

'Oh?' he said.

'Well,' Harry said, only partly aware of how irritating

Maddie found him, 'I mean, I ended up teaching. You know, *those who can do, those who can't . . .'*

His voice would have trailed off, and he would have taken a sip of his beer to fill the conversational void he expected. Maddie, we can imagine, clenched a fist, like a boxer.

'Actually, I admire you,' Jonathan said, turning to him. They both remember this, the way Jonathan said it. And the way that Jonathan looked at him, Harry says, it was like he was appraising, quickly appraising the length of Harry's body and then allowing his gaze to rest on Harry's face as if he was looking intensely at something interesting through a microscope. And Harry's breath, it unexpectedly caught, this is what he says. And even recounting it causes him some embarrassment, because it was at that moment, he says, that it started to strike him. It did. It struck him that no-one admired Harry Logue. It struck him that he led a life lacking in any admiration at all. He knows it's inexplicable that he reacted, that he must have been visibly taken aback. He knows it would have been easy to have interpreted the comment as patronising, or the look as sinister, but he didn't. And, of course, we weren't there, we didn't hear Jonathan's intonation, see his face, feel what passed between them. It's not for us to judge what was in those words, or that look. But it took a noise, someone laughing, someone somewhere over to their left, to break the spell, apparently. Harry looked, and as he did, says he caught sight of himself in a mirror. He remembers he seemed to look hungry for approval somehow. A bit desperate. He says he straightened his back and rearranged his thoughts, but his reflection that night remains with him. If you ask him, he'll tell you.

For Maddie, her memories of that night are coloured differently. The more she is forced to remember, the tighter the grip of fear. What prompted her to speak to Jonathan was more to do with herself. That night she says she seemed to feel more sensitive, physically sensitive. The material of her dress felt odd against her skin and she remembers the sensation as melting spasms of prickly pleasure. Prickly pleasure. And she says she didn't want to share them with Harry. She's clear on that. When she entered the hallway of Oakhall Manor, she admits to suddenly feeling an inexplicably acute longing to be desired, and even the touch of her own fingers against her face, her hair, her forehead, seemed intensely promising. She would tell you that Jonathan Cotard happened to be the first man she saw. At first she says she thought there was something familiar about him, and she felt she had no choice but to speak to him. To her, the conversation comes into focus only after what must have been a clumsy introduction. Maybe it was because she felt Jonathan looked only at her eyes, yet seemed acutely aware of the rest of her, that sustained her interest. Maybe.

'It's cold outside,' she remembers saying. 'It must have rained solidly for a week.'

'Yes,' Jonathan said, fully attentive. 'Where have you travelled from?'

And as she answered, Maddie recalls the smoothness of it all, the cadence and conceit of it, the way she felt no discomfort. She concedes that Jonathan was a handsome choice. Tall, poised. She remembers being just about to ask him, in a roundabout way, if he was alone or with company, with a wife, perhaps, when Harry and Gerald's son invaded. Harry, with his expectant smile and pint of beer. Harry, with his jeans and jacket and sticky hands and his irritating necessity to have to alert everyone to the fact that he was a bloody teacher. Jonathan, she felt, handled Harry well. She remembers the conversation-stopper.

'Actually, I admire you.'

Maddie says she looked at Jonathan, and at that moment,

says she saw what she needed. Was it his wisdom and experience? Was it his tone or timing? His money? Or was it just a need for those long fingers of his, for his skin? And suddenly she says she ached. That's how she describes it. Like a pain. As if it was a pain she hadn't felt before.

As if.

'Jonathan,' she said, 'you must tell me what you do.'

'What I do?' he said.

'For a living.' She would have sounded breathy.

Without realising, she says she had rested her hand on his and as he answered, she felt the warmth of his skin on her palm, and a trickle of adrenaline raced downward. She had his full attention again, and she remembers correctly: he had a strong face, long jaw line, hair greying at the temples a little, but still dark. She remembers she became aware of the groove of his jawline, his neck and of the outline of his collar-bone through his shirt.

He sensed it, she says he did.

'. . . so I'm not here very often now unfortunately. My work is mostly in the States . . .'

She had thought he was familiar to her, but now she wasn't so sure.

'. . . last saw Gerald five years ago . . .'

Maybe the voice was familiar. She couldn't be sure, and anyway it didn't matter. Words didn't matter. Nothing mattered to Maddie, then.

'Dad was proud of you all.' She remembers Gerald's son summing it up, smiling too innocently.

Maddie says she snapped her hand away from Jonathan, aware of her own desperation. She knew Jonathan had noticed it. Felt sure of it. She says we'd have been able to see his realisation if we'd looked closely, if we'd been there. She tried, so she says, to make it dissolve but its imprint was there.

Maddie will admit all this. She'll admit that it's hard for her to describe the stalker-like terror she felt as she waited outside the gents' toilet later on that night. Harry, still self-deprecating, would have lost sight of her again and it was Jonathan she waited for in that smallish, darkish, out-of-the-way hallway. A dead-end hallway, with only the gents' toilet at the end of it. She remembers it was like waiting in a grave. And when he appeared, superficially taken aback, he would have read her face, her body, and when they spoke she says she knew it was impossible for her to turn back and impossible for him to ignore her. She says it all haltingly, stopping mid-sentence – sometimes mid-word – as if she's lost something, lost confidence maybe. She would have us believe she had no choice, that when she kissed him, when they stood kissing in that dead-end of a corridor, seedy though it might appear, this only heightened the feelings she had for herself. Maddie remembers not a Mills & Boon moment. Far from it. She remembers his smell, of soap and something like citrus, not recognisable or particularly pleasant to her. She remembers the pressure of his hands on her body, the clinical nature of their unfamiliarity. She admits to hoping someone would catch them, see her with her maroon dress hitched up around her waist, see flashes of her skin, her thighs. She remembers feeling the strain of her calf muscles stretching against the tip-toe stance, and the shock of cold wallpaper rubbing against her shoulder blades. She remembers the deftness of Jonathan's response. Cruelty or kindness, she wasn't interested in either really. She just needed what she needed. Something more than she had. And she says she remembers someone, one of them, him or her, saying, whispering something. 'Open your eyes, look at me,' something like that. And feeling him closer and harsher than her own breathing.

That's Maddie Harper.

That's Maddie Harper all over.

We have to wonder, don't we? We have to wonder if she was thinking about anyone but herself, if she ever considered anyone other than herself. But that's the thing about Maddie Harper, she doesn't think. She doesn't think about consequences.

And Harry, he says he knew nothing of this. He's shocked. Hearing it makes him shocked. Even now, knowing all he knows. Amazing. What he says is he was with a crowd of people he vaguely remembered but didn't like. He says he was getting tired, but felt good. He says he didn't know where Maddie was, and he didn't realise Jonathan wasn't there. His voice cracks a little as he tells us but, listen, we don't need to feel sorry for him. Or her. Both he and Maddie have their demons, both of them. And whilst Maddie gathered herself together with a quick glass of red and a secret cigarette, Harry says he was enjoying the feeling of being admired. That's what he says. He says he felt admired. And admired by Jonathan Cotard. He says he would have liked to speak to Jonathan a little more, find out some more about him – where he lived and so on – maybe arrange to meet him again. Ironic, but yes, he says he thought he would have liked that. He says he realised something that night. A flash of realisation about what he needed. He says he was re-running things in his head, trying to click ideas into place when Maddie appeared. Most people had drifted off by that time, and Harry remembers she seemed to arrive into the room as if from nowhere.

'Where've you been?' Harry said, out of habit more than anything.

'Talking,' Maddie said. 'Why?' And he remembers her walking on ahead, towards the exit.

Harry says he couldn't think of an answer. That was the

truth of it. And he says he felt in his pocket for a coin and pulled out a 2p. He remembers flipping it in the air and catching it.

'Heads or tails?' he said. It's ridiculous to think he tells us this in all honesty. He says he remembers Maddie standing holding the door open, looking at him painfully.

'Tails,' she said, and Harry says she sounded tired, or bored.

And he slapped the coin onto the back of his hand.

Heads.

He says he remembers Maddie shaking her head and walking out alone to the car park.

And there it was. Decided. Or so they both thought. Both of them say they thought it was over, for sure that time. Both of them say they thought, again, they couldn't possibly go on like that. That's how it should have been. Not for the first time, both of them with their different reasons. But they're not so different. Not really.

And as they walked out to the car that night, they might have thought it was the end of something. The end of it all. Harry, all bolstered up by being admired by a stranger, and Maddie, temporarily rejuvenated by her own foolish desire. Both of them feeling brave.

Idiocy.

That's what it was.

And, of course, they were wrong. It wasn't the end of something, actually, it was the beginning. A beginning. Another beginning.

Maddie remembers her car was one of the few still on the car park. Covered in a sheen of glistening frost, she remembers it looked a little spectral.

'Shit,' she remembers saying, and it was because of the prospect of clearing the ice.

'I'll do it,' Harry said, and whilst he scraped the windscreen with a credit card, Maddie got in, started the engine and would have shivered against the blast of air from the vents.

It's true, the night was frosty; Maddie recalls watching the stars appear as ruptured pinprick lights in the blue-black sky as Harry removed the ice from the glass in strips. She could see her breath clouding the glass on the inside and says she was momentarily reminded of Gerald's funeral and that cold church. And her irritation at Harry, she says, came in swift waves. *Hurry up*, she thought. *Why's it taking you so fucking long?*

'Come on!' she would have snapped as Harry flicked ice from the edge of his credit card into the air.

And Harry got into the car. They both remember the air inside was just beginning to warm. Maddie says he reached for his seatbelt, stretched it across himself and clicked it. She says she was watching him, she says she was leaning forward in her seat, one hand on the wheel, the other on the gear stick. She says she could see the white of the skin on his knuckles but his face was indistinct inside the darkness. She says she heard her own voice as if it was a voice squeezed out into the black air.

'Christ's sake, Harry. How long does it take you to do a simple task?'

She says she wanted to set up another ending. An absolute ending. She wanted him to dare to answer, to dare to argue back. She wanted to force things. But she remembers how still, how quiet he was. Maybe it seemed like he wanted this ending to be on his terms.

'Well?' she said.

Still nothing.

'I could have done it quicker myself,' she said. And even now, she can hear the clumsy immaturity in it all.

Harry, she says, stayed quiet.

'God.' Maddie would have revved the engine, shoved the

gear stick into first gear and, when she drove off, they both say the car snaked a little on a patch of ice, jolting both of them. Harry must have sighed or breathed out too heavily; that's when Maddie says she seized the moment. 'And don't start complaining about my driving. It's the bloody ice.'

It's all so predictable. It is, really.

And again, so they say, the car jolted, the engine complaining a little against another patch of ice.

'Just let me drive,' Harry said. Maddie says it was as if he couldn't contain himself any longer and he reached for his seat belt clip.

'No.' Maddie now, grateful for the chance at an argument at last, swung the car off the car park and into the lane.

'Let's just get home in one piece.' Harry said this quietly, probably still trying to keep things on his terms. 'Try to be careful.'

It doesn't take much imagination to work out this was exactly what Maddie wanted. *Try to be careful*. They both agree this is what Harry said. Something about being careful. And Maddie would have been so keen to have seized upon every syllable.

'Careful? In one piece?' Maddie says she was yelling by that time. 'Christ Almighty, Harry. Would you prefer to bloody well walk?'

'No, I was just saying . . .'

'Well don't. Don't *just say*.'

We can imagine how the light from the headlamps was beginning to ripple too fast across the hedgerow lining the lane.

'That's part of your problem, Harry.' Maddie admits she was in full flow by then, and as she pushed the gear stick into third gear, she said something like, 'But you've got so many problems, haven't you?'

She says whatever it was she actually said, Harry seemed

suddenly affronted, wounded, and said, 'What do you mean exactly?'

And just as suddenly, she remembers starting to laugh. Maybe her anger was exhausting, maybe she was a bit hysterical. Maybe it was the thought of getting her freedom back, reclaiming it again, leaving Harry, again. Whatever, she says she threw her head back, felt the headrest hard against the back of her head, and laughed. So when she turned to look at him, when she took her eyes off the road and said, 'You're asking me what I mean? Oh, come on, Harry, surely with your encyclopaedic knowledge of human behaviour, you can work it out.' That was the moment that Harry snapped. She says that was the moment.

Harry remembers feeling a mix of irritation and a painful need for revenge. At that moment, he says he just wanted to choke her. He really did. He wanted to grab her neck and squeeze the laughter out of her. Squeeze the life out of her. He'll admit to this. And he'll tell us he was only vaguely aware of the speed they were doing, only partly aware of the pitch of the engine and the periodic catch of the tyres against the grass verge and the flickering scratch of frosted hawthorn, or whatever it was, against the side of the car. And he says he made a grab for her. One of those baffling, risky reactions. He doesn't remember actually grabbing her, actually touching her, but he will concede he might have at least surprised her, frightened her, given her the impression he might really hurt her. At the time he says he just wanted to shock her, just shut her up. If taking hold of her hand, or her neck, would quieten her, then good. This is what he thought. And he remembers hearing her gasp. And it was then that it happened. Or at least this is when they say it happened. Whether we believe them depends whether we trust them or not, really. They say that at first they thought they'd missed the bend in the road, mounted the grass verge, hit a fox or a badger. That's what they say it felt like, a sort of bump or a bit of a knock, a scrape of metal against something. A thud. And a flash of something maybe bouncing off, left, into the hedgerow. And Maddie stopped. She says she stopped straight away. Braked and stopped the car. Drew it up tightly against the hedge in that thin lane. And they might have sat for a second, less probably, with the engine idling and headlights illuminating the lane at an acute angle, so nothing looked straight. Both Maddie and Harry must have been aware of their heartbeats, their breathing. Both will admit they weren't absolutely sure what had happened. Not then.

Maddie got out of the car first, and Harry, climbing over her seat, struggled out after her. The lane was shiny with damp or ice, and they could see the tracks the car had made. It was easy to see, right there, how Maddie had misjudged the bend, bumped up the verge and off again.

'Your wheel hub's over there.' Harry said, and they both walked towards the glint of silver in the hedgerow, tramping over slippery grass and mud. For a moment they say they felt relief.

'It's here.' Harry said, and stooped down to get it.

Maddie says she was the first to notice. She says she noticed whilst Harry was recovering the wheel hub. She speaks as if some astral light shone down and illuminated a dim shape of something lying among the grass and weeds. At first, she thought it could be a bag of rubbish, a black plastic bag flung out in the country lane by a fly-tipper – that's not so unusual round there – but as she approached, she says streaks of pinkish industrial light flickered across the blurred outline and, with an increasing realisation, Maddie says she could make out the shape of a body. A human body. A man. When she looked, she could see there was no blood. She could see he lay, basically prone, his legs angled awkwardly somehow.

Something was odd about his jaw, she could see that, and a bluish bruise – bluish in that light, anyway – seemed already to be forming, covering most of his forehead. What Harry remembers is her screaming, and he remembers looking up from his vantage point and seeing her. He says she had the look of a Victorian madwoman, a silhouetted shape, screaming without pause. Just one long breath. He says he raced to her, over the hardened mud and earth and nettles or whatever they were, like a child running into the sea. She was still screaming when he reached her, by this time on her knees beside the body.

'Look,' she might have said. And Harry looked. He looked at the bluish skin and long fingers, the good-quality trousers, the odd but still recognisable jawline, the greying hair at the temples.

'Fuck,' one of them said, maybe Harry, 'it's Jonathan.'

Maddie remembers Harry saying something like 'He's not dead, you can see his breath.' But it was her breath coming out in bursts, hanging above Jonathan's body. Maddie's breath, closer to him than to her. And they say they didn't know what to do, how to squeeze his wrists to find a pulse. They say they were unaware who was still screaming. Maddie remembers looking up, though, and when she looked up, Harry was some distance away, crouched against the hawthorn.

'Harry,' she eventually called, 'Harry, what shall we do?'

But Harry wouldn't have been able to hear her, he says he could hardly cope with the sour, beery vomit that just wouldn't stop, and the sweat, which despite the frost, was running down his back. So when Maddie appeared next to him, he knew the look he gave her was pathetic, and without speaking, they say they ran back to the car and Maddie drove off.

They're not particularly proud of themselves. Not really. They knew it wasn't the right thing to do, they knew it was a mistake to leave.

It was all a mistake really. All of it.

They say they didn't speak in the car. Maddie claims she had regained her composure enough to run on autopilot. She remembers thinking about him, seeing his face at the reunion, feeling his skin against hers. Jonathan Cotard. One of Gerald's successes. Jesus, the thought of what they'd done. Re-running it in her head: mounting the grass verge, Jonathan walking along the lane – who knows why – then looking briefly behind but having nowhere to go before being hit, probably being dragged a little way through the nettles and weeds. She couldn't help herself imagining what Jonathan's last memory might have been, the pain he must have felt. The terrible pain. The rawness of the terrible guilt of that pain. That's the sort of torture she would have put herself through as she drove back home that night.

And we can imagine how they didn't look at each other during the journey home. Maddie, keeping her hands clamped to the wheel – she might have cried if only she could, instead she kept to the speed limit on roads that seemed hopelessly long. And somehow, crossing the border into the Black Country – welcome to it – would have seemed, to her, like driving right into Hell.

It's easy for us to judge. Easy for us to be judgemental. But we mustn't be mistaken. Both knew that night their lives were changed forever, that nothing they had done before could match that. Nothing. Both probably thought it couldn't get any worse.

But we've already marked them as flawed thinkers, haven't we?

Let's not philosophise about that now. Not now.

If we could have seen their faces as they arrived home,

probably wheatish and pinched in the glow of streetlights, we'd have laughed. Maddie probably rushed into the house first, but Harry says he hung around outside for a while, a bit like an extra on a film set, or playing the part of the unknown voyeur. He says he watched as Maddie flicked on lights, closed curtains, flicked off lights. It could have been twenty minutes or more. She'd have closed the front door after her, as if she didn't expect him to go in, and Harry says he felt his heart ache as the cold bristled against the wetness on his cheeks and chin.

Maddie hadn't locked the car, and it was parked with two wheels on the pavement, skewiff. Harry says he thought he ought to move it, get rid of it. He says he felt acutely aware of beginning to plot his defence. When he crept into the house, he says Maddie was upstairs, lying on the bed. All lights were off, so it would have been that grainy type of darkness that allows you only to see things accidently through the corner of your eye.

'Maddie,' he would have said from the bedroom door, 'Maddie. Give me your car keys.'

And when she didn't answer – he knows she'd have heard him, but didn't answer – he flicked on the light. Maddie curled further up and covered her eyes. Imagine it. It was then that he thought he heard her say something but couldn't make it out. Stepping towards her, he might have said, 'I need your keys.' And although, to him, Maddie didn't seem to move, he says he heard her say something like, 'I don't think so.'

Harry says he stopped in his tracks, and slowly, really slowly, Maddie sat up. He recalls the electric light bulb seemed to be buzzing a little as if it was in danger of going out at any second, and it cast a sort of forty-watt light over Maddie. He says her make-up was smudged and smeared, her hair hung limp. And she squinted against the light.

'Give me the keys. We'll have to get rid of the car somehow.' Harry remembers this, moving closer to her.

'Leave it,' Maddie said.

'No, if the police . . .'

'You're not getting rid of the car.'

Harry says he sat on the edge of the bed and they seemed to look at each other for a long time. Only when Maddie looked away did Harry say, 'What did we do? Tell me what we're doing.' Something like that. And he says it was then that she swung her legs off the bed and said, 'I'm going to take a shower.'

Maybe that was her intention, to take a shower, to wash him – to wash Jonathan – off her, but Harry caught hold of her wrist. They both remember that.

'Take a shower?' he said. 'What do you mean?'

He says she seemed to look down at his fingers around her wrist, too tight, and tried, weakly, to twist away from him, but he didn't let go. Not then. Not then. These weren't his terms.

'Tell me. Tell me what we're going to do.' Even Harry could hear he was whining. Whining and holding on. And she, Maddie, she wouldn't have been able to cope with that. She absolutely wouldn't have.

'Get off me.' And we can imagine her twisting herself, plucking at his fingers, beginning to feel the static collection of blood in the veins of her hand. 'Don't, Harry.'

'Don't what?' He says he was more than likely standing now, and with a swift movement, says he grabbed her shoulder with his free hand, and she fell or was pushed suddenly backwards against the wall next to the window. We can imagine that in the speed of things, her bedside table was shoved over and we can guess their feet scrambled against the mess of books and lipsticks and pens. They say their faces were almost touching and Harry says he remembers feeling his hand stray towards her neck, pressing his body against hers, so they must have looked like they were in the midst of some kind of grotesque dance, or like some single figure, oddly contorted. Harry says he felt her thighs weaken under the pressure of his hips and was momentarily caught by an unexpected softness around her belly. People say this kind of thing happens at moments of great anxiety. It's all about how excitement turns in on itself somehow, that's all. But Maddie remembers feeling Harry's breath on her face and thinking for a second that he would kiss, or kill, her. She says she'd never seen him like this, never realised he was quite so brittle. She claims to have heard a rasp and knew it was her own attempt at breathing, and then remembers feeling a lightheaded sense of departure, or something, and then quite suddenly, Harry let her go.

Actually, she says now she wishes he'd killed her. She does.

'Where are you going?' she managed to say as he left the room, but he would have ignored her. He would have heard her, but he probably couldn't trust himself to speak. Not until later.

And it must have been couple of hours later that she went downstairs to the kitchen for a glass of water. He was sitting in the semi-darkness and she says she was initially struck by the vinegary smell, unsure it if was him or the drains. Without a word, she splashed some water into a cup and says she drank it in one go in front of him.

'It was your fault,' she thought Harry said, and he wasn't looking at her. 'What?' She remembers putting the empty cup down on the work surface and turning to him.

'Last night. What happened. Last night. It was your fault.' Harry was sitting at the kitchen table. Maddie says his legs were tightly crossed and his hands were clamped as if in prayer between his thighs. He must have looked and sounded tightly wound.

'My fault?' Maddie's voice, raised, probably.

'Yes. I know you'd had a drink last night. I could smell it on your breath.' Harry says he didn't even try to control the contempt in his voice.

'Could you now?' Maddie. Imagine her advancing on him a little. 'Oh right. Would that have been when you were trying to beat me up in the car, or later, when you were trying to strangle the life out of me?'

She says Harry seemed to loosen, and his head dropped. She'd got him. Again. Easy. She says he looked down at the table, seeming to become acutely aware of the knots and fibres in the pine. At any moment, Maddie says she expected him to cry, or something.

'I'm not taking the blame for this,' Maddie would have said. 'If you're looking for someone to blame, look at yourself. You can't control yourself. You caused it. Look at you. What are you even thinking?'

She says she sat down opposite him, leaned across the table. She knew he'd be able to see the blue blooms of bruising around her neck in the growing light of the morning. She wanted him to see she hadn't slept. She wanted him to see it just by looking at her eyes. And, she says, in a rush of faith, or something, he reached over and touched her face with just the tips of his fingers. And she says she didn't even flinch.

She remembers watching him speak.

'I know what you think of me,' he said. 'You think I'm a loser. Everyone thinks I'm a loser. I spend every day fielding off crap from adolescents sugared-out on chocolate spread who all think I'm a loser. And then I come home. To you.' She remembers he might have hesitated. 'And you treat me like shit.'

And she knew what he meant. And she was thinking, it's true. She knew he was remembering that day, years back, when she'd left him. She'd left him, and just as he was getting himself back together, she'd come back. To him, she'd come back just to treat him like shit.

'Christ.' Maddie says she felt angry, says she rocked back against the work surface. 'What the fuck does that matter? Why is everything always about you?'

Then she maybe straightened up and walked over to the window. Their garden is visible from there, and it would have been bruised purple by the early light. She might have been reminded of Jonathan – of his forehead, of the colour of his skin. She might have run her fingers across her neck, sore and bumpy. 'Your self-pity doesn't explain last night,' she remembers saying, but quietly.

Harry, of course, had wanted sympathy, he'd wanted her to yield to him a little. He says he wasn't ready for her coldness and got up quickly, says he remembers the sound of the chair scraping across the tiles on the floor. Hard against hard.

'You'd had a drink. I could tell,' he said. 'And you were driving.' He says he squared up to her. 'You were driving.'

It's astonishing really. Astonishing that they were having this conversation. Why weren't they calling the police, or an ambulance or something? There was still time.

'Really?' Maddie would have sneered, let her eyes flick across his face like she was searching for something impossible to find. 'OK. I tell you what. I'll take full responsibility and then you can feel so much better about yourself.'

Harry says straight away he didn't like where this was going and felt himself diminish a little. He says he doesn't like conflict. Isn't good at it. So when Maddie gets like this, when he can see her getting like this, he can't deal with it. It's beyond him.

'Hey, I know,' she would have carried on, sounding mad, like a mad woman, speaking louder and louder. 'I'll call the police now and I'll explain exactly what happened. I'll tell them how you grabbed the wheel of the car whilst I was driving, how you'd been drinking, how you were sick at the scene, oh, and, of course, how you tried to attack me, kill me, later.'

She says she made off towards the hallway, as if towards the telephone. Harry says he followed her, protesting. He'll tell us how they grappled with the telephone, how their voices mingled discordantly, of the 'he said/she said', of the self-indulgent crisis defence.

We could guess this argument, this baffling set-to, this fight, could have gone on for some time but what stopped it was not guilt or regret or evil or pain. None of that. It was the doorbell. One single note ringing through the hall, and suddenly they must have been in suspended animation. Eyes wide. Freeze-frame.

'Fuck,' Harry probably said.

'Don't answer it,' Harry says Maddie hissed.

The doorbell again. Like a hot needle. A hot note. It must have been like someone resting their finger against it without respite. Harry would have been the first to move. And even though Maddie apparently objected, he opened the door. And cold air would have swept in, a promise of snow. And there, standing outside with his finger still pressed against the doorbell, apparently, was their next door neighbour, Paul or Phil or Alan or somebody. It must have taken a moment for Harry to register that it wasn't the police.

From what they say, this neighbour wasn't pleased. 'Your car,' he stepped sideways and motioned towards it. 'It's blocking my drive, mate. I have to go to work, I'm on earlies.'

Maddie says she stepped forward and remembers the way this neighbour looked at her.

'Jesus. Hard night?' he said. Something like that.

And it was true, in the light of the early morning, Maddie

looked a mess. Still in her red dress – maroon – standing in that doorway, she looked a mess.

'I'll get the keys,' she said.

Neither of the men said anything, and Harry didn't look but would have heard the shuffle of her bare feet on the stairs. Obviously, she wanted to show all was normal, give the impression it was all OK, but he knew she didn't want to get back in that car. When she appeared, it was with an impassive look on her face. Apparently, she said nothing, so there would have been one of those stagey silences, and then, according to Harry, she walked down the path like someone with cramp in one leg, all awkward, lopsided, generally off-balance. He says she looked like someone who had suddenly experienced a kind of ageing spurt usually brought on by stress, or children. He was most likely right. And both men watched as she got into the car, started the engine, moved it a foot or two back and sat with the engine running.

Now free to leave his drive, maybe their neighbour seemed more affable. They say he waved at Maddie. Walked towards his car and waved at her. But they say something made him stop. Something made him stop and stroll towards Maddie's car. She says she watched as their neighbour strolled towards her, his head angled sideways as if he was scrutinising something. For a second, Maddie would tell you she felt a sudden urge to drive off. She says she could have done, he was advancing towards her with such stealth, he could have thought she hadn't noticed him. But she says she stayed put, we can imagine half-curious, half-terrified at what might happen next. She says he stopped and, head still tilted, pointed at her headlights as if drawing an imaginary horizonal line in the air.

'Your headlight's broken.' She says he looked concerned.

Maddie was paralysed, she must have been.

'This one.' He pointed to the near-side light. Then, turning his attention to Harry, said, 'Fucking kids vandalising the cars at night again. Had mine done last week. Little bastards. I'd let the police know if I were you.'

According to Maddie, he left, shaking his head, raising his arm in thanks or whatever.

Just so that we know, when Maddie and Harry first met, it was a spring day. Maddie will say she remembers little of it, little about him, except that she thought he looked like a tramp, in need of a shave, was a bit thin, wasted looking. Their second year at university would have been nearing its end and they'd somehow managed to avoid each other on campus until Gerald scheduled meetings with them to talk about dissertation proposals, or whatever. One of them, probably Maddie, had misread the instructions on Gerald's memo and had arrived uncharacteristically early. The door was closed. So Maddie and Harry remember they stood quite awkwardly together, in silence, both unsure they were in the right place, so they say.

Harry will have us believe he remembers that day vividly. He gives a surprisingly sophisticated account of his impression of Maddie, what she wore, how her hair was styled, the smell of her, the sound of her voice, how she moved, how she sat in the easy chair in Gerald's room. He says she looked like an arty type, a bit of a feminist, maybe, or the type to be into Buddhism, the sort of woman who might have a sketchy tattoo on her hip or buttock. She didn't, of course. In fact, she wasn't – isn't – any of those things. Harry will tell us how he was aware of trying to soften his Stourbridge accent during their conversation with Gerald, says he didn't want to appear parochial or working class to her. Says he didn't want to be himself in front of her. Says she brought something out in him, even in that first meeting, that made him feel hypersensitive somehow, about himself. And as the three of them sat together, Harry says he made up his mind that he'd like to pursue her. The idea came to him gradually, maybe like salt melting in hot water rather than a bolt from the sky. But we know the promise of what lay beneath her flimsy cotton dress was enough to make him believe he might be in love or something. Typical Harry.

Maddie is less forthcoming. Her memory is stained with time and resentment. She doesn't say it exactly, but she seemed to view Harry's translucence with disdain. To her, she says he looked a little desolate, untidy, worthless really. Not her type. She says she could tell he was a local lad with conventional ideas, just the type she worked hard to avoid. When she talked about her interest in 'images of womanhood in early twentieth century literature' she says she noticed how his eyes widened and how he had, a little insincerely she thought, tried to reinterpret some of what she said. Gerald kept them on track. She remembers bits of the conversation.

'Images?' he had said, 'Do you mean *representations*, Madeleine?'

'Yes, I was thinking that,' Harry said, too enthusiastically.

But Maddie says she wasn't sure that was what she meant. She wasn't sure at all.

'And why stick to twentieth-century literature?' Gerald had continued, lighting a Rothman's. 'Why not look at some earlier writing?'

'Absolutely,' Harry said – that's the sort of thing he says even now – 'I mean, Madeleine, you could look at Aphra Behn – or even the Bible . . .' She says she thought it odd he should use her name like that, unaware he was just trying out the sound, her sound, the sound of her in his mouth. Harry's like that.

And so this is how they met. So, maybe this was the start of it, in Gerald's room with its worn brown furniture and lethal smoky orange hue. Afterwards she, Maddie, went her way, towards the city, undoubtedly meeting friends, probably nothing much planned; he, Harry, probably invigorated by the discussion, would have headed directly to the library having booked a carrel for private study. Unbelievable that they ever got together at all really.

Apparently, it was a couple of weeks later that their paths crossed again, almost end of term. Harry remembers it vividly, wants to recount it. He says he'd decided to go home. Sounds like he travelled for miles, doesn't it? Actually only a few. Takes less than thirty minutes, even on the fairly dodgy Black Country public transport. So, Harry tells us it was a Saturday. He remembers feeling a nagging doubt about an essay he'd handed in. Some philosophy module he hadn't quite understood. Something about morality or whatever. He says to take his mind off his anxiety, he'd taken a walk into town. This is the town he – they – still live in now. Yet look at how he talks about it. He says he walked past the bus station, through the subway and then up into the town he felt sure hadn't fundamentally changed in hundreds of years. Yes, there were cars and single mothers with buggies and a shopping area with a fountain, but Harry talks about it like this – and we have to agree – he says if you stripped away all that 'metropolitan glaze', underneath was the grime of industry and a certain attitude of self-preservation and something like despair. That's what he says. To him, it leached out from every paving slab, every bit of tatty flapping bunting, and wheedled its way into the flat vowels and creeping intonation. At once a dead and alive place. And all its glass-making, chain-making, chain-smoking inhabitants looked basically the same to Harry on that day. All of them old before their time with perilous expressions, thinning hair and lardy, fleshy midriffs. These were Harry's thoughts as he walked through his home town that Saturday, past the bargain clearance shop, the building society, the tiny jeweller's; past the pub with the almost inevitable all-male clientele spilling out onto the narrow pavement, holding pint glasses of cloudy flat beer, and talking in surprisingly high-pitched voices with thin own-rolled cigarettes glued to their lips; past the ugly dog-walking, pot-bellied women with head-scarves and no teeth; past the youth of the town, mental kids with asymmetrical eyes and crew cuts and nits; past the girls, crowds of them – what is the collective noun for this type? Posse? – posses of girls with dyed hair, too much mascara, and piercings clearly visible in parts of their bodies not meant for public display, whose command of English would only ever remain as enclosed, as limited as the area would allow. Harry admits he slowed to look at them. And one of them, a girl who looked about fourteen going on forty, seemed to spring out from the crowd, stopping Harry in his tracks. This part, ac-cording to Harry, is important, because as a reflex, he held up his arms, palms outwards, and skipped back. The girl, having been shoved by a heftier friend, first giggled, then feigning sudden disgust at the thought of being thrust into the open arms of a complete stranger (and more particularly, probably a stranger who looked like Harry) said, 'Ewwww,' and squirmed away, to the delight of her pals. According to Harry, as he walked on shaking his head, he heard the girls shout 'Perv!' or something like it. And right at that moment, just as Harry was receiving the full brunt of adolescent rebuke, Maddie ap-peared. Actually she emerged from one of the many charity shops, but to Harry she just seemed to appear in front of him, like an angel. Behind him, according to Harry, the tirade of abuse was reaching fever pitch. Maddie would have heard it, he says, she obviously saw him, felt a reaction, felt the un-justness of it. So, Harry says, throwing her arms round his neck and kissing him whilst simultaneously giving those vile girls the finger seemed the best reaction in the circumstances.

Maddie, though, was a chancer – still is, really – and as she stood on that narrow grey footpath with her recently bought secondhand bangles clanking against the nape of Harry's neck, she admits she enjoyed it. The pleasure was in the suddenness of it though. Nothing else.

Harry, of course, couldn't believe his luck. And when Maddie released him from her grip, he predictably asked if she wanted to go for coffee. Unsurprisingly, he'd been sensible with his student loan and there was a quiet café run by evangelical Christians at the top of town. He thought she might like that, but even before he had a chance to suggest it, he says Maddie whispered, 'Take me somewhere.'

So he did.

He'll tell us he took her back to his room in the attic of his parents' Victorian terrace, all the time half aware that it could be a dream, that he might wake up in his single bed in his digs in Wolverhampton and it would all have been a fantasy. Because he had been fantasising about her. Often. Although he'd looked for her on campus, he never saw her. Having made a decision to pursue her, his attempts had fallen flat. Had he known where she was though, in the bars and pubs, he probably wouldn't have had the courage to approach her. Not Harry. What he had ideally wanted was a chance meeting in the library or somewhere, or maybe Gerald would invite them both for another meeting. Harry. He's always been such a loser.

It's no surprise that Maddie was the first and only girl he had ever taken back to his room at his parents' house, or that he'll admit that he was instantly, totally and utterly convinced that she was 'the one'. The one. He's just such a soft touch, Harry is. Too easy. People walk all over him. In a way, he brings things on himself and then wonders why people take advantage. It's like he's testing people somehow, testing their morality. And, to be fair, Maddie's come to enjoy ridiculing him. She says she slipped into an arrangement with him during a bit of a dry patch on the boyfriend front, and through his persistence and her guilt (yes, she calls it guilt) they sort of stayed together. We can see it, can't we? We can kind of see it.

In truth, Maddie hadn't particularly intended much more than a quick fling with him. Once, maybe twice would have been fine. She's never been much of a planner. She says planning drives her mad, but she would have liked to have travelled a little after university, done some volunteer work somewhere maybe, written a novel perhaps, seen what happened. She thought Harry would be like the others and would just sort of fade out of the picture, no need to give him the push. Easy come, easy go. But somehow, she says, a pattern began to emerge between them, and even when the other lads – those inevitable end-of-term goodbyes – disappeared, Harry seemed always to be there. Her constant companion. Good old Harry. Always there. Looking hopeful. Hopeful, or something. Sometimes, she says she wondered if he knew about the others, but not enough to ask him. She never asked him about anything, not until recently of course. When she left him, just after they'd finished their degrees, she vowed she'd never to go back to him. Never. Said it was over between them. Said she'd travel a bit. Maybe do something useful with her life.

She ended up back with him, though. She'd been away from him for less than a year. Not even twelve months away from him.

That says a lot about her. And him.

It would be good to report that, driven by guilt or compassion or something, Maddie and Harry did something constructive, maybe called the police or an ambulance to help Jonathan. We might expect that maybe something other than themselves, their own self-preservation, might have pushed them to try to put things right. But it didn't. Not immediately anyway.

When Maddie returned from moving the car that morning, as she brushed past Harry in the hallway, he says he heard her say, 'This is all your fault.' Harry remembers her tone, acidy with reproach, her eyes burning. He would have wanted to bite back, but at the back of his mind he would have wondered if she had a point. Passive, woolly-cardigan old Harry. So he didn't reply immediately, and there would have been a silence, one of those painful ones. Imagine how the draught in the hall would have made him shiver a little, and how he might have shoved his hands into his pockets. Maybe his fingers closed around a 2p coin. Maybe he took it out of his pocket, looked at it.

'What're you doing?' Maddie remembers asking. She knew her voice sounded heavy. She remembers she was sitting in the kitchen. Her legs crossed. She remembers she was fiddling with her hair, and Harry knew what that meant, so felt brave enough to say something like, 'No Maddie, this is your doing.'

'But I stopped straight away. I stopped the car. I got out.'

Harry said he felt the coin, hot, in the palm of his hand.

'Yes, so?'

'You were sick, Harry.'

'You should have done something to help him.'

'You were sick. You vomited, right there.'

'You should have tried to help him.'

'You didn't help me, Harry.'

'We could have done something. Could we? What could we have done?'

They don't remember precisely what they said, but they do remember they were soon quiet again, both of them hemmed in by their own thoughts. And Maddie explains it like this: she says it all without emphasis. It's as if the words leave her mouth at precisely the moment she thinks them. As if it was quite simple. She says she apparently said something like, 'You ran back to the car first Harry, you left first. You left him there first.'

Harry doesn't remember leaving first – leaving him, Jonathan, first. He doesn't remember who left first, but that's the funny thing about memory. If we try hard enough, we can forget things, erase events, or become blind to what was there. Just as easily we can exercise a complicated filling-in or topping-up of events, imagine things that didn't happen, see things that weren't there. It's almost like a primitive instinct. We can find another perspective, another viewpoint. How can anyone be sure what's true and what isn't, really? But somehow, in the confusion of that morning, a decision was made to return to the lane, to return to the scene. Let's assume it was some attempt to put things right. Maybe. Let's assume that.

Both of them were probably groggy, exhausted really, still in last night's clothes. Both of them were probably afraid, nastily reluctant. Both remember the damp, rusty morning air stinging them and clinging to their skin and hair as they got into the car, though. They remember streetlights randomly pinging off, and, low on the horizon pencil-thin lines of daylight dimly marking the start of another day. Listening to them, it almost seems as if there was a curious sense of connection between them on that morning, there in the car with its wonky headlight, with Harry ashamedly aware of the red angry marks on Maddie's neck, and Maddie's nauseous solitary confinement.

The day wasn't clear – to them, it wasn't clear – just cold. Very cold. Driving up the shallow slant of a road, as they had the night before, Harry has confided that he took a sneaky sidelong look at Maddie's legs. He'll actually admit to this, watching her calf muscles tensing and relaxing with each frequent gear change. Good legs. Maddie, unaware of his interest (so she says), strained and slowed to see, to make out where they'd missed the bend, squinting into the hedgerow, past nettles and twigs.

'Where was it?' she said, and Harry will tell us how he continued watching as she braked and her red dress rode up a little on her thighs.

Desperation has a strange effect on people. It turns us inwards and forces us out at the same time. And perhaps that's what they were, what they are: two desperate people lurching through the stodgy landscape, not knowing what to think. And not knowing what to say they thought.

The lane was deserted. This is true. Maddie slowed the car so that there was only the throb of the engine to hear, until she said, 'Was it here?'

Harry says he wasn't sure, says he told her he couldn't remember where it had happened. He says he thought the lane looked different in daylight. It's true, it did look bleached out, a bit desolate. Maddie says when she got out of the car and started walking towards the hedgerow, she felt they couldn't be far from him. Not far from Jonathan. Who knows what they were expecting, maybe an airborne arrow pointing the way or a convoy of police cars, an ambulance, maybe. Wishful thinking. And as Maddie set off again up the steepish curve, Harry says he followed her, says he told her, 'Slow down.' He says he'd noticed something: tyre tracks on the other side of the road. Black tyre tracks which had cut through the frost, up and onto the grass verge. Maddie says she saw them then. Misty clouds seemed to droop over the hedges, over the lane, over Maddie and Harry. They both say this.

'I don't remember the church.' Harry said, 'Maybe we're in the wrong place.'

Maddie says she stopped, squinted to her left, at the cone of a church steeple just visible through the dampness some way behind oak trees.

'No,' she said, 'this is it.' And, according to Harry, she just seemed to slide out of the car.

And he watched her as she did. He says he thought she moved a little like a cat. He could see she was determined, so determined that she'd left the door of the car open and the engine running. He says she looked quite suddenly young, very young, and just for a split second, he was reminded of something, someone. And as he followed her, he remembers feeling his heartbeat shudder through his arms and neck and stomach, and thinking he might be sick again. He would have swallowed hard a couple of times and closed his eyes. When he opened them – and it was only a moment later – he saw Maddie standing on the grass, her back to him. He says he felt a compulsion to go back to the car, move it, park it somewhere safe. Good old Harry, always trying to thinking sensibly. So, whilst he stood, shuffling his thoughts, Maddie stood feeling the cold air scrape her skin into goose-pimples. She could surely see an imprint of the night before through the dried brown weeds and frost. Could definitely see tyre prints, a confusion of footprints, a flattening of grass and weeds. She must have known that if she took a look near the hedge she'd see the vomit that Harry had left behind, as long as the foxes hadn't got there first. She traced the trajectory of last night's journey with her eyes, and she says her breath came in sharp white bursts. She surely must have seen the tyre prints, the footprints, the flattened grass and weeds. Again. The tyre prints, oily against the frost, the scattered footprints and broken grass. She stepped forward, looked closer. There they were, she said she saw them, the tyre prints, hardened with the cold now, a crazy dance of footprints or body prints, divots of grass and soil missing and various flora and fauna squashed down grey and black and yellowish.

And that was it.

That was all she could see.

Then Harry was next to her. And they both say it was like the night before, with the two of them standing, looking down and then across. It was like the night before, but not exactly.

'Where is he?' one of them said, maybe both.

Harry says he stepped forward, stooped down, ran his hands across the frost on the grass. Maddie, following an impulse, crossed to the hedge – you can understand why – she couldn't believe it, she wanted to check. So she kicked some leaves or sticks to one side, and there was Harry's evidence, Harry's vomit. They were in the right place.

They were in the right place. But there was nobody there.

No body.

Jonathan, he wasn't there.

She says she looked across at Harry, who seemed to be conducting a fingertip search of the area on his knees now, stroking the earth.

'This is definitely the place,' she remembers saying. And they say they looked at each other like they hadn't done in a while, because little by little something like relief had begun to wash across them both. Relief and gratitude and hope and happiness loosening the grip of fear. And Maddie called to Harry, she did.

'He's not here,' she was saying. 'He isn't here.'

And, though it wasn't the intention, it must have been a little like when they were younger suddenly, like it had been all those years back. And she says she fell to her knees beside him, Harry that is, and kissed him. It was the relief that did it. The relief and gratitude at the thought of getting away with it. And weakness. Of course. They're both so weak.

And what a picture they would have made, there on the grass verge, clinging to each other like they were drowning, flattening the weeds even more with their knees, unaware of the cold and damp, maybe beginning to believe they were in the clear. Who really knows what they thought happened. That they'd imagined it all, maybe? That it was some quirky joint hallucination? How ridiculous. Life isn't like that. It really isn't. They know that now, of course, but right there, clutching each other, they probably thought they'd experienced a kind of period of totality. A sort of evil-minded positivity.

Thinking about it now, it was a pleasant outcome.

But what fools.

Naturally it didn't last for long. Moments really. If that. Seconds. And it was Maddie of course, Maddie who spotted it first. If we ask her, she speaks as if it just seemed to appear, right there among a tangle of crooked ivy. Harry says he felt her grip on him change, and for a terrible second – that's how he described it, a terrible second – he thought she'd seen him, Jonathan, lying there broken. Broken because of them, because of what they'd done. He says he felt her inhale quickly, he felt the spread of her shoulders and straightening of her back beneath his hands. Suddenly their faces were close, nose to nose almost. Both were searching each other's expressions, each other's features, for clues. Harry, probably looking pinched, almost ferocious, air leaving his nostrils in rapid spurts, afraid to break the gaze. And Maddie, drunk on her own adrenaline, saucer-eyed and, what's it called? Her overlip? No, her overbite, making her look like a rabbit caught in the headlights.

People are funny, aren't they?

Almost in unison, they say they both let each other go, and Harry says he watched, stupefied, as Maddie stretched her hand into the knotted weeds. He couldn't look at what she'd found, he says he just couldn't. Instead, he says he was concentrating on her face, on her bluish skin and how gusts of bitter wind blew wisps of greasy hair across her forehead.

He says he noticed she'd lost an earring and uselessly thought maybe that's what she'd seen, maybe that's what she was reaching for. Evidence, he says he was thinking, don't leave any behind. Maddie was looking at something in her hand then, and still Harry says he couldn't look to see what it was. He was afraid. We know that. Harry's always afraid. On edge. But at that moment when it must have seemed to him that all his demons were colluding against him, he must have been terrified. And Maddie, she didn't say anything, not at first. What had she found? What was she turning over in her cold hand? It's obvious if we think about it. Something inadvertently left behind. It was, of course, a wristwatch. Gold. A little grubby, some of the strap missing. Gold hour markers. And the words *Patek Philippe, Genève* in plain text on the simple blue dial.

Harry says he watched as Maddie held it to her ear, the one with the earring missing. Maybe she heard the faint click of time. The faint click of the night before.

She looked at it, then held it out to Harry. 'It's almost 7.30 already,' he remembers her saying, her eyes dulled with tears and her face slack. To him, then, she didn't look like Maddie.

'Fuck. Is it his?' Harry said, but he didn't take the watch from her.

Harry says Maddie's body slumped as if she'd been hypnotised, or punched. Harry, on the other hand, says he was disproportionately energised, instantly restarting his fingertip search of the area.

'Maddie, come on,' he said, 'help me.'

But Maddie, she was crying. Not for Jonathan, she's perfectly honest about that. No, she was crying for herself. She was crying for the hope that had been snatched away. She says she was crying because she'd lost faith.

'Come on,' Harry kept saying, 'he must still be here somewhere.'

He says he could feel the cold mud oozing into his shoes and through the material of his trousers. He says he could smell the sharpness of winter; it hurt his nose and his throat and cut through his skin. He says he felt the urgency of the day pressing down, says he thought surely if they didn't hurry, they'd be seen, by churchgoers if no-one else. He didn't know what time church services started, but somehow he felt he just couldn't leave. Not now, not now, he kept thinking. And anyway, he'd left the keys in the car, they could make a quick getaway if they needed to. He says he didn't really know what he was looking for any more. A body? Really? He remembered the night before, how Jonathan's face had looked so horribly wrong, how there seemed, at the time, no chance, no possible chance that he could have survived.

Maybe he had though.

Maybe they'd got it wrong. Couldn't he have just got up and walked off? Couldn't he have recovered and walked home? Dropped his watch in the confusion. But they had just left him, hadn't they? Hit and run, that's what it had been. A cowardly thing to do. Cowardly and evil. What kind of people were they?

Harry says he started to shiver uncontrollably. He couldn't feel his fingers. Says it felt like there was no blood in his fingers, or his hands or feet or knees. Saliva or tears, or something, was dripping off his face onto his hands as he continued to search through the undergrowth. He would have felt disgusted with himself. Seriously. Really disgusted.

'Help me, Maddie,' he said to her. 'Come on.'

But he says when he looked round at her, she was still slumped on the grass, looking down at her own hands.

'Maddie!' He would have been shouting now. 'Fuck's sake, help me.'

He remembers she raised her head to look at him. He says

she had the expression of a woman about to take aim at a dartboard.

'Stop looking at that fucking watch. Look for him. Look for Jonathan now,' he said.

It might have been that an abrupt tiredness had overtaken her, and although she might have tried to speak, he says her speech was slurred with cold. She made no sense and only shook her head.

Harry's very clear, though. He says he felt a familiar twinge of anger and, rising to his feet, walked unsteadily over to her. Her hands were in her lap, and Harry could see the watch-strap. He says he crouched down and took her by the shoulders.

'Stop looking at that watch now,' he said. It was his teacher's voice.

He says when she shook her head he felt his jaw clench and grind. He would tell you that what happened next was out of his control. A limbic reaction – some fancy term or other – but whichever way you cut it, Harry struck Maddie. Across her face. An open-handed slap. Quite hard. Hard enough to knock her sideways. Hard enough to surprise her into opening her hands to save herself, to release not only the watch, but something else she'd just found. Something else that had rested within the nettles or thorns nearby.

The watch flipped out of Maddie's hand onto the grass, and alongside it, a wallet. Leather, obviously, and black. Maddie says she'd seen it at almost the same time as she saw the watch. She says she opened the wallet as Harry had conducted his own search. She says inside there was a business card, some credit cards, some loose change.

Harry scrabbled to pick it all up, not yet struck by enough guilt or remorse at hitting Maddie – that would come later. As he rifled through it, the wallet, driven by disbelief or something, Maddie stood up. She says she did. The skin on her cheek would have already looked crinkled into crimson, and chapped, and the way she would have looked at Harry, not intimate any more. More like he was a stranger, an enemy perhaps. Yes, like they were enemies operating some kind of truce. A ceasefire of silent disdain. Not exactly hatred. No. Much more than that.

She says she reached down and scooped up the watch, then took the wallet from Harry's limp hands. As she did, a coin fell out. She just remembers getting up – it was a struggle – and walking towards the car. Harry says he watched her. He says he noticed the stains on her dress, a patch or two of darkness spreading into the red material, and her legs, he noticed her legs were smeared with mud, reddish brown. He thought she looked a mess. No, he didn't feel any guilt just yet.

Harry says he watched her drive away, and then he saw a coin on the patch of earth nearby him, a coin he'd seen fall out of the wallet. Even from where he was standing, he could see it was a two pence piece, coppery orange against the soil. He says when he looked closely, he saw it had landed on heads.

And Maddie was gone.

Harry says he didn't go straight home. It's true that he let himself crack a little. He cried. He did. He'd crossed the lane and walked up the slope, by that time, hoping that Maddie would return to collect him, to forgive him. By the time he reached the church, it was clear to him she wasn't coming back and he says he felt his heart sag. *Forgive me*, he had begun to think as he wandered into the cemetery. He had so much for her to forgive. So much more. And the bells, the church bells were already ringing, and Harry says he leaned against a yew tree and, at that moment, thinking he was totally alone, closed his eyes. He says right then, at that moment, he wanted to remember everything clearly. He wanted his old memories to somehow block out the new ones. It was the guilt. It was a sort of tumbling of guilt. It does strange things to people. And he did remember. He remembered Maddie wearing a white dress, cotton, something floaty and not quite see-through. Her skin, pink like she'd been in the sun for ten minutes and, as usual, had forgotten to put on sun-block. To Harry, that moment, that memory is so clear. He'll say, he'll tell us how in his memory she's smiling one of her open-mouthed smiles and running towards him. He'll say he can hear his pulse throbbing in his head. He's nervous and hopes he looks handsome, rugged. He wants to catch her, to hold her. He can't wait to feel the heat of her skin – anticipation is something like an adrenaline rush – and he can't seem to catch his breath. Behind her a sun is setting, peachy against a dreamy horizon, gradually silhouetting her so that he can't make out her expression any more. And then it's like a film ending and she never reaches him and he never does feel her warmth or manage to touch her. She fades away and suddenly he's a diver reaching the water's surface and his consciousness overtakes his desires. He takes a cold breath and feels his eyelids flicker.

Then she's gone. Everyone's gone, or so it seems. And there he is – was – there was Harry, back to reality, back in the cemetery, eyes wide open, standing amongst the gravestones. Grey stones. Stones with dates and cliches. Hard, cold endings. Harry remembers there was a sort of hum coming from somewhere, he didn't know where. He didn't care. He says all he wanted was Maddie then. He says it was like a bolt of realisation. He needed her. He needed her to wash away the memory of what they'd done – what he'd done. But even though he closed his eyes again, he says he knew she'd gone, faded out. It was just a memory. A hope of a memory. And he says he knew she'd never be able to forgive him. Never. How could she? And he'd probably never be able to forgive himself.

Good.

~

There was a lot of blood, that's what Maddie says she remembers most. A lot of blood and unbearable pain. It happened when she got home.

She had headed for the bathroom. The house, she says, felt grimy, especially the bathroom. She remembers stepping over a thin towel lying like a dead animal – a drowned animal – on the floor. Discoloured paint and dusty skirting boards gave the place a sour, scummy feel – according to Maddie, an emblem of Harry's broken promise to make it good. Maddie said she felt like she was noticing things for the first time. She'll describe her disgust at the dried droplets of water and soap on the perspex shower doors, the clump of hair caught like a web across the plughole. She'll tell us about the brown water in the toilet bowl, someone's dark pubic hair stuck to the rim of the toilet seat, the fact that Harry had left the seat up. Again. She says there was a halitosis-like smell coming from somewhere. We get the picture. At that moment, she was much more sensitised to it. She says she felt a sense of both connection and disconnection, of looking out and of seeing inside herself. She says she felt ashamed.

Standing there, still holding the wallet and the watch, she remembers vividly, very vividly, the way the sharp slanted winter sunlight cut across the room like a searchlight, looking for her, missing her and instead illuminating cobwebs heavy with dust in the corner where the wall meets the ceiling. Then she remembers catching a glimpse of her reflection in Harry's shaving mirror. She says she looked panicked, sharp, guilty. She says she noticed for the first time a short but deep vertical line imprinted between her eyebrows. Even when she tried to lighten her expression, its ghost remained. She says she pushed her hand through her hair and it felt tacky. She says she wondered what had happened, what was happening to her. *Yesterday I was Maddie Harper, estate agent, in control-ish, solvent-ish. Look at me now.* Fact is, if we chose to live the way she does, in that type of Hell, it would change us. It just would. She must have looked closer, leaned forward and looked. Very close. She says what struck her was her lips, bulging and full liver-red. Pre-raphaelite, someone had apparently once said. Men like her lips. They do. Some actually mention them when they talk to her, or about her; others can't seem to take their eyes off them. Solicitors, clients, builders. Doesn't seem to matter who they are. So, there she must have been in that scummy bathroom of theirs, looking at her own face, and she says she suddenly shivered, just quickly. She says it was the memory of the night before. Jonathan's lips, the feel of them on hers, the unfamiliar taste of him. And a sharp, tingling sensation spread through her, like ink on blotting paper. Not quite pain. No, not really. And she says she was aware she was trembling. And she remembers closing her eyes then. Both she and Harry, closing their eyes. What a hapless gesture. Everything was still the same when they opened them. She says she was still loosely holding the watch and wallet, and without really thinking, dropped them, and they fell next to her feet. And she says suddenly the feeling of hopelessness was stifling. It's pathetic really, but in a gesture of remorse or something, Maddie says she flung open the bathroom cabinet, quickly scanning the contents: half a bottle of Gaviscon, three opened blister packs of paracetamol, a pack of safety razors and Harry's hairbrush. Not enough to kill herself with. Yes, she says the thought was crossing her mind. But only fleetingly. She'll tell us now that she would rather have killed Harry at that point.

Oh, Maddie.

She's says she's trying to be honest.

And of course, the thought of Harry would have flitted

through her mind then. That bastard Harry. Yes, she would rather have killed him at that point. She says she remembered him on his hands and knees on that grass verge, wasting time, when it was clear, patently clear to Maddie anyway, that Jonathan wasn't there. What the hell was he thinking?

God, she hated him then.

At that moment she did. She says she wished it had been Harry she'd run over. Killed outright. Painfully.

She says she looked again at her reflection. Says everything behind her was in shallow focus. Her neck would have been reddened and sore looking, but her face would have held no sign of the slap she'd received. She'd have thought that was a shame. And so this must have been why she did it.

She says she reached into the cabinet and picked up the hairbrush – Harry's wooden paddle hairbrush. She says she noticed her fingernails, her nail polish, remnants of it, blue, bits she hadn't quite removed; her hand, grubby, dirty with soil and grass stains or something. She must have watched as her knuckles whitened as she gripped the hairbrush. Then with one circular sweep of her hand, she says she slammed it, the varnished hard wooden side of the brush, into her face, her cheek, so that the force of it jarred her jaw and split her lovely lip. And she watched her own expression change. The shock, the throb, the bloom of bursting blood vessels, the instantly damaged, angry skin.

Blood must have dripped down her chin.

She must have looked like a vampire then. An angry, hurt, lovely vampire.

And it's that about Maddie. That, right there. That dark, Black Country in her. That's what gives people hope about her. It is.

And she said she was shaking when she put the brush back

into the cabinet. Shaking when she looked at her misshapen, swollen face again. Her smile would have been lopsided. And she would have thought it was good. Painful, but good. She would have thought she deserved it. A quick, sharp pain. But if anything, she says the pain seemed to be increasing, not ebbing away as she had expected. And it wasn't a throb any more, she says it was more like a jabbing, twisting sensation, a real stab right down her neck, her shoulders, through her chest, down, down into her belly.

She says the grind and push worked its way down her thighs. She says she trembled violently. And without warning, she says, she doubled over in pain, aware that the epicentre wasn't her face, it was her belly, her groin. She says she felt light-headed, woozy; the world, she said, looked black and white. She says she could hear a heart beat, it might have been her own. She says her legs moved unsteadily and she felt her feet slide on something sticky. When she crumpled to her knees, she saw it, all the sticky. And her face would have plopped down hard against the cold blue lino. The last thing she remembers, the last memory she had before everything dissolved around her that morning, was the sheer amount of blood which had run – was running – down her legs, covering her feet, and forming a corona of dirty red around the wallet and the watch.

That's what she says she remembers most vividly.

That, and the utter relief of it.

Harry says he gawped at the church, realising she wasn't coming back for him. It's medieval or something, the church is. Beautiful building. It stopped being imposing many years ago, though, and its tower – its spire with a bell – is part of the landscape. Taken for granted. It's a goodness just beyond most people's reach. It really is. And we all know that the only people who go there now are old folk trying to reserve a place in Heaven, most likely apologising for a life of mistakes at the last moment, mouthing hopeful prayers, becoming more desperate in their certainty that there's more to life than this. There isn't, of course. This is it. This is all there is. Every rational person knows it. Any God, or Universe or whatever could only be indifferent. We're born, we live, we die. End of.

So, Imagine Harry, too young and too early, looking at the church door. He might have been tempted to enter, to confess or something, confess a couple of mistakes. But he says he didn't. Instead he says something about a cat – a black one – that seemed to appear from nowhere. A stray. Says there was a mouse or a bird in its mouth. Says he could see it was still half-alive. Could hear it was alive – this bird or mouse – making some pathetic movements and noises in that cat's mouth. Harry says he just remembers walking away, his back probably hunched in that way he does.

It had probably just started snowing by the time he was out of sight.

She says it seemed like an indelible mark. Try as she might to wipe it clean, she couldn't. She'd woken up where she had fallen on the bathroom floor, cold and panicky at first. Soon calmed. The watch beside her read 8.07 and somewhere in the distance she could hear the D sharp of a persistent single church bell. She had risen to her feet, says she remembered it all. As if it had happened to someone else. Remembered it like a film. She'd removed her dress and let it drop into the pool of blood – her blood; had watched her skin prickle with the chill and, naked, had wiped and rubbed away at the blood on the floor. She had, breathless, watched it smear and soak into her dress, a towel, tissue paper, a sponge, but even though she tried, the floor didn't seem clean. Not really. She said she ran a bath, and soaked herself. Says she watched the dried blood mist from her into the water like a ghost. And the relief. The relief was a comfort. And afterwards, clean and blushed with heat, she placed a towel on the floor to cover the marks only she could see and watched the snow falling like limp paper against the window.

Harry says he thought he had hypothermia by the time he arrived home. As soon as he let himself in, he says he could smell Maddie had had a bath. He says the house felt warm and he felt a moment of foolish elation, or something, and closed the door loudly behind him, stamping the snow off his feet. He says he took the stairs in twos, and steam rose from his arms and legs. The bathroom door was open and, to him, the room looked clean and fresh. He says there was a tacky warmth about it, condensation on the window, a single damp towel on the floor. To him the room smelt good. To him the room smelt of Maddie. He stopped and breathed it in.

And then he says he thought *where is she?*

In a rush, he says he threw open the bedroom door, and the room was dark, the curtains still closed.

And Maddie's bits and pieces, he says, were scattered about the place. The upturned bedside table, the unmade bed, the memory of last night. There it all was. We've pictured it.

'Maddie,' Harry would have said, hopeful she might be there somewhere.

He would have opened the curtains, Harry would, he would have seen that outside it had stopped snowing, but the sky sagged grey. To him, the street might have seemed dead. He would, most likely, have seen his footprints crunched into the snow; uneven marks approaching round the corner, past the neighbours' houses, past the lamp post, across the garden, right up to the door. But from his high angle he would certainly have been able to see another, smaller set of footprints leaving the house and, at the kerbside, where Maddie's car should have been, a shaded, snowless rectangle, and tyre marks where she'd driven away.

At first, he says he thought she'd left him, again. Says couldn't help himself. This was always his first thought. He says he tried to stop himself from reliving that moment fifteen or so years back when he'd come home and she wasn't there. She'd gone, left him.

And he wanted to tell her. To confess. He did, really. But there was just Harry and four walls. White walls in a dark room. And white sheets on a hard bed. And there was that hum, still coming from somewhere. Harry says he thought then: *I don't know or care what's happened, I only really care about you, Maddie.*

He'd wanted to tell her then, to explain. Right then. Right at that moment. He says he did. Not that he cared about her. No, not that. Not then. He says he needed to tell her about something else. He says it had seemed like the right moment. He says he knew he had to do it. Maybe it was just a culmination of guilt. He's full of that. Full of it. But he thinks he knows her so well, even now. He does. And he truly believed he could give a good account of himself. He honestly, truly did. And he says he had a plan – that's exactly what he says – he says he had a *plan*. A plan of how to tell her. He says he would have taken her hands, looked straight at her and said, 'Look, I did something.'

'What?' she might have said.

'Something I'm not proud of, something I need to explain,' he would have said.

Then he would have told her.

It was his *plan* to tell her.

He says he would have told Maddie how it all started. How he first saw the girl waiting at the bus stop, scrawling something into the mist of spray, rain and breath on the perspex shelter. He would have said how, as he drove past he could see that she had traced a heart shape with her finger. He would explain how he made a point of driving past her every morning for weeks, increasingly fascinated by her and, actually, by his own behaviour. He would certainly tell Maddie it felt like a compulsion, out of his control, and when, on that rainy morning he stopped and offered the girl a lift, he had already rehearsed every possible dialogue, not wanting to appear like some loser desperate to pick up a young girl. Harry knows he's not much of a catch – and let's face it, he isn't – but he thinks he's not bad looking by today's standards, and all women are impressed with a flash car, aren't they? So he'd have hoped Maddie, of all people, would understand. Maybe, he would have thought, she could have helped him understand why he did it. Because that's what Harry is like. He thinks there's an explanation for everything. Even now.

Despite all this, he must have known he'd be taking a chance. He'd have told Maddie he had no idea this girl, this beautiful girl – and she is beautiful – would get into his car, fling her school bag onto the back seat and laugh. It's true, to Harry she looked different close up, older maybe, or familiar. He'd have described the way she wore her hair in a ponytail, tied loosely off her face as if she had nothing to hide. And when she sat in his car that first time, quite literally steaming from the cold rain and smelling of soap and damp cotton, he knew it felt right. Of course their meetings became a habit. Harry and this girl. Every day, for who knows how many days, he would collect her from the bus stop and drive her to school – not his school of course, he's not a fool – and every day she, this girl, revealed a little more about herself, and gradually that initial glottal chink of adolescence widened into a beautiful confidence. She was a bright spark, she knew things beyond her years. She said she thought the pointers and clickers had replaced the movers and shakers of Harry's generation. We have to love her arrogance – Harry sort of did – and he says he knows Maddie would have liked her, *really* liked her, this young girl. How ironic. She wanted to be a doctor, travel the world, she was top of the class, gifted in a way, yet to Harry, she somehow seemed to have everything and nothing in equal parts, a symptom of the miscalibration of youth. To Harry, it was probably her immature, directionless energy that was so compelling. In his heart, though, he says he felt Maddie would understand, and because of this he says he'd have explained how he wanted to give this girl something – something to kind of ground her, help her somehow. He says he would have told Maddie about the gifts he gave this girl. Little gifts: a bracelet, a book, a 10cc CD to make her laugh because she told him his taste in music was like her dad's. He says he'd tell Maddie how he noticed the girl wore a little more make up each week – nothing tarty, quite subtle and quite beautiful really. According to him, it was as if they were giving each other gifts, courting each other in a very old-fashioned way. And it very quickly became clear, absolutely clear to Harry, that it was meant to be. Harry believes they were both victims of pace, he and this girl, and he felt if he didn't seize the moment, close the deal, he might have blinked and missed it. So when he collected her that time and said 'Do you want to skip school, come with me for the day?' and she smiled and nodded, he knew. He says he knew she understood, despite her years. It seemed a natural progression, a good thing, a necessary tightening of a ligature.

Harry says he would have been very careful about explaining the next part to Maddie. Says he would have been diplomatic, evasive. Says he'd have told her how they went to a hotel, but not which one. Says he'd have told Maddie how he made the girl take her school tie off before checking in, leave her blazer in the car. Says he wouldn't have said how impressed she was, or how excited she was or how she giggled as they entered the foyer, holding his arm as if they were newlyweds. Says he wouldn't have said how much he liked the feel of her or how he squeezed her to him as they checked in as Mr and Mrs, or how young he felt, or how he stole a rose from the arrangement on the Reception desk and presented it to her between his teeth.

He says Maddie would have needed to know how they sipped mineral water – sparkling – in the room. Harry, considering himself a doggedly decent man, would have definitely told how he had refused the girl's requests for champagne. Champagne. He refused that request. Harry says he knew the whole situation required an under-commemoration and he wanted to give the girl only some illusion of control. Of course she was free to leave whenever she wished but he justifies it to himself by saying he didn't want her to be authority-intolerant. Harry was, after all, still the adult and was well aware of that. He must have been. And he isn't stupid, he's a great believer – as we all are – in behavioural flexibility and is well aware that people change their minds and doors are closed forever, but he says he'd have tried to make it clear to Maddie that he had lost something to this girl, she had already taken something from him. And in that room, in those four white walls that afternoon, in that hotel, on those crisp white sheets, he'd needed to take it back. To him, it was a need.

The fact that she was eager and that he found it hard to believe it was her first time is something he says Maddie wouldn't need to know, and he says he'd have couched this information in sensitive terms; he says he'd probably have told her that girls mature so early these days, that he didn't hurt her, this girl, that she said she loved him – she actually used those words – she took Harry by surprise, he says that wasn't what he'd had bargained for at all. But he says he'd think twice about admitting that she cried afterwards, how there was nothing he could do to stop the tears – great howling tears. He says he'd stay quiet about the fact that he didn't know what to say or do and would say nothing of how they eventually just dressed, and how he took her back; of the wordless car journey; how he drove her to the bus stop, and how he kissed her one last time and how, strangely for the first time, her dental orthodontics jarred against his own teeth; how she felt different to him somehow, limp and empty. He says he would admit that everything she, this girl, had said suddenly felt alien, everything they had done was undone, disintegrated. He says he'd confess he just wanted her to get out and close the door, but she stayed and clung onto him and there was a cheesiness about her skin – something he hadn't noticed before. Little black smudges of mascara had collected in the corner of her eyes and her lips looked bluish in the failing light. And, to him, she suddenly looked like that young girl tracing hearts into the air. Harry says he might have admitted that little by little he had felt the confines of his car closing in on him. In fact, he says he wanted her to just get out, fly away and live her life. *Go on*, he says he'd thought, *be a good doctor, travel the world with your friends, get a life, but get away from me.* And as she leaned against him, her hair greasy-damp with tears, he says he'd felt repulsed by the smell of her. A cat-food and chemicals, salty, thick smell, a smell of childish sweat, of guilt and regret. He says he'd felt suddenly quite sick, claustrophobic, dizzy and remembers looking down at her legs and her laddered tights and bony knees, and at that moment felt a jolt of remorse. He says he'd felt like the kind of man he hated: a cheat, a liar, the kind of man who would examine your underwear whilst you were out. *Don't worry Maddie*, Harry says he thought, *at that moment I knew exactly what I was.*

68

Harry says he remembers the girl saying 'Goodbye, I'll see you tomorrow.' And he remembers it sounded more like a question, a hopeful high-rising tone, so he'd said 'Yes, same time, same place.' And must have felt himself redden against the lie.

What he says he'd definitely have told Maddie was that when the girl left him that day, she never looked back, not once. He might have craned his neck to see her disappear into the distance and she would have looked just like any other school kid returning home from school. The sway of her hips might have looked somehow off kilter, maybe a little gawky. For Harry, he says he would have been clear: that was the end of it. No more hearts and flowers.

Just having to remember this, to re-run it, reduces Harry to a wreck. *I'm not what they say I am.* He says he thought, *I'm not. You know that. I'm just tired. I want you, Maddie, I want you to be here, at home, and I just want to be close to you.*

This is what Harry says he was thinking.

Good old Harry.

But when he looked, he'll tell us he could see their suitcases still balanced on top of the wardrobe and her shoes still piled in the corner of the room. And when he opened a drawer, he says he pulled out a pair of her knickers, felt the material – not silk – and brushed it against his lips, feeling it catch on his skin. He says he remembers reaching into his back pocket, getting his mobile phone out, calling her and leaving her the message she's still got saved. 'Hi, Maddie, it's me. Where are you? Come home. I'm home now. We'll talk. I want to talk, I do. We can sort it all out. Come home. I'm here now. Just come home.'

And he would have sat on their bed and waited, praying in his own way that Maddie would come back.

But Maddie, as I say, Maddie was with me. She didn't know

what to do. She's beautiful when she's needy. And we have a connection. Yes, that's what we have. She didn't stay long. She never stayed long. I said to her, I said I'd help her, there was no need to go to the police, really there wasn't. She was upset, crying; so was I by the end of it. And that gave me something. Hope, maybe. So when she left me, drove off and away, I knew she'd come back. She had to. She always does.

She's a user is Maddie Harper. Always has been.

But two can play at that game.

By the time Maddie arrived home, the snow had turned into grey, driving rain. Harry says the first thing he noticed about her was the bruise, dirty blue on a face set, grim, tight-lipped. The guilt must have descended on him like a virus, and even before she reached him, he would have been saying something like, 'I'm sorry Maddie, I am.' But he remembers Maddie sidling past him, arching her body away, not wanting to catch the virus maybe. But Harry persisted. He says he followed her through the house, imploring her, and then somehow they were in the kitchen, and he was standing too close to her, trying to hold her – actually trying to take hold of her – and he says she seemed to be squirming away from him. He says it was killing him, he was desperate to hold her. And his hands were on her arms, her shoulders, then her face, his fingers, tracing the bruise, and all the time, he says he kept telling her he was sorry, so sorry. Even though she twisted her face – her body – away from him, he persisted with it, he kept on with his sorries until she had to respond. And she did.

'Shut up.' Just a whisper through lips too tight, and Harry says he stepped back. It must have been as if he'd been unexpectedly released from a trap, as if he'd realised she was breakable. A china doll. And when they looked at each other, Harry says it felt like it was the first time in ages.

'I'm so, so sorry,' he said, the words mouthed almost sound-lessly. 'I never meant to hurt you.'

Maddie's gaze didn't falter, her breathing was deep, and Harry says he felt a flicker of relief or something.

'I love you, Maddie,' he told her, and he says he stepped forward, trying again to hold her, and though she resisted at first, Harry says it seemed less than before and he felt he'd caught her again, and he held her to him, breathing in a dirty urban smell on her hair and skin. He wanted to tell her then. He wanted to tell her his little secret. He wanted to, but he says he was thinking *Where has she been?* even though it didn't matter to him then. And he was probably saying her name, whispering it to her, and he must have felt her hands on his arms, his elbows, not resisting but holding him steady. And he would have felt brave. Brave enough to tell her about the girl, brave enough to whisper 'Maddie, I think I'm lost.' And he says she felt hot against him. 'Just a little lost.' Then she said something he says he didn't catch, and he says he released her just enough to look at her face. He must have thought she'd be tearful, upset perhaps, but her face, he says it was set hard, and it must have taken him aback for a second.

'Lost?' she said. And Harry says he let go, all relief must have been evaporating.

'What does that even mean? Why do people even say that?' And she maybe seemed to propel herself away from him.

'I know,' he said. 'I just feel . . . I don't know what I feel. I just don't.'

He says she made a move to leave but he stopped her, grabbed her arm. He wanted to tell her.

'We can start again,' he was saying. 'It'll be good. I'll be good, I promise.'

'Shut up.'

'We can sort all this out. We can.'

'Shut up.'

And Harry was most likely matching her step for step as if they were in the midst of some complicated ballroom dance, both of them stuck on repeat. Visualise it now:

'Maddie, don't.' (*left, right*)

'Get away from me.' (*right, left*)

'Don't go. Just stay. I need you. I don't know what to do.' (*left, right*)

'What to do?' (*together . . .*)

And then maybe they were still.

Maddie apparently moved back awkwardly. Harry says she looked odd. He says she took a step back, opened a drawer without looking and pulled out a knife – not a sharp one – and held it out to him.

'Here,' she said. 'Do it.'

And he says she was handing it to him. Handing him the knife. It wasn't even sharp. And she was shaking, a look of terrifying want on her face.

'Do it,' she said, but she was looking at the knife, watching him take it from her. At that moment, he believed she wanted it all to be over, he really did. And Harry, he says he was thinking *where has she gone, my Maddie? Where has that carefree girl gone? What happened to us?*

Truth is, if you choose to live like this, in this type of Hell, it changes you, it just does. Of course, Harry says he dropped the knife. And the act of it, the sound of it, metal on the stone floor, jolted the moment. And he says Maddie gasped, as if breaking from water.

'We have to get a grip.' He can say it now the way he said it then, as if his chest hurts from breathing.

'Yes,' she said, but it took a while. 'Yes, we do.'

And he remembers her nodding, too slowly, saying, 'We have to find out where he is.'

And he says she was shaking. Trembling.

Harry admits he was struck by the sound of her voice, her flat Midlands vowels, flatter than usual. Flat and lazy. He says it was as if it she was drugged. One word running into another, running into another. Like she was drugged, or exhausted.

'What do you mean?' Harry says he tried to touch her shoulder but she moved sideways, away, and he caught hold of her sleeve with his finger tips.

'Well, he can't have just disappeared.'

'But he has.'

'What?'

'Just disappeared.'

Maddie, let's imagine, would have seemed to shake herself loose. 'Fuck sake,' she might have said, or something like it, and she might have stepped forward, past him, avoiding the knife on the floor.

'Where are you going?' Harry said, his tone would have been desperate again.

'To find out where he is.'

And, according to Harry, Maddie was a shadow in the hallway then, beginning to rummage through coats, hanging up.

'But how . . . ?' Harry says he trailed after her, watching as she rejected coat after coat, then finding one, slid into it, shrugged uncomfortably and shook it off onto the floor.

'Maddie, how?' He knows he was whining again, and Maddie, he says, seemed to be deliberately ignoring him, testing how far she could push the silence. How many times had they played this game? Not enough, just yet.

Harry says he remembers Maddie turning to him square on. He says her eyes were straining, burning.

'We have his wallet, we have his business card,' she said. 'We know his address then.'

She paused, and Harry says a look of cruelty crossed her face, and she said something like, 'I'll go there, see if he's there, or someone's there. Someone might know. I'll drive there now.'

Harry says he moved towards her but she was already opening the door.

'You can't be serious,' he said.

'I am.'

'You've got it the wrong way round, Maddie.' Imagine, his hand on the door, the skin and flesh of his wrist puckered.

'And you think you're always right. Why won't this door open?'

'No, I don't.' His knuckles, they would have been whitening against the brass door handle.

'Christ, aren't you sick of being so right all the time. Let it go, Harry.' He says she looked like a trapped animal – like a trapped cat – and she was tugging and pinching and scratching at his arm. 'Because I'm sick of this.' And she was saying this and pulling, scratching at his hand until he let go, defeated. 'I'm sick of you.'

They both remember a raw wind sweeping in from outside as she pulled the door open, and mini twisters of hazy rain swirling round into puddles on the slabs. Harry says he watched her hunched figure blur off down the path. Without really thinking, he says he stepped out and called after her, 'We should take my car if we're going to do this.' And he says Maddie turned and blinked at him, blinked her burning feline eyes and was almost wet through already. 'We should take mine,' he said, quieter. 'Yours is . . .'

And although she would definitely have been kissing the edges of anger, when she sat in Harry's innocent, unblemished Audi, she would have been able to see his point.

Harry blasted the heater. He says he did.

'You're cold. Have a blanket,' he said. He was trying to

normalise it, trying to make it right. Trying to calm it. And he says he leaned across to the back seat, grabbed the tartan blanket and spread it across her lap.

'I'm fine,' she said, fumbling through the wallet – Jonathan's wallet – and, apparently, with cold fingers, dropped the business card, watched it tumble between the seats, sideways into the foot-well behind. Maddie says she cursed herself, but reached round, bending and stretching like some kind of contortionist.

'I'll get it,' Harry said.

'No.' Maddie remembers unfastening her seatbelt, switching round, kneeling on the leather seat, reaching down and round, remembers feeling her fingers gripping the card. And she says she remembers thinking how tidy Harry's car was. No grit or grime, no empty containers. A place for everything. A box of tissues, a road map, a bottle of water. Tidy. And then she says she saw something. On the back seat. She remembers seeing it. A blazer, a school blazer. Polyester, dark blue with burgundy piping round the lapel. On the pocket, easy to see, an emblem of ropes and a lion, and just visible an embroidered name tag at the collar. Embroidered. The sort good kids have. Good parents sew them in. Just too crinkled to read, so she says.

'Got it?' Harry said.

Maddie says she twisted back into the seat. She says she answered automatically, but her mind would have been calculating. And as the rain turned into sleet again, she says Harry drove northwards towards the city.

See, Faith.

She went missing on a Monday. Autumn was turning to winter. Short days, closed curtains. The police were calm.

'Don't panic,' they said. 'We'll send someone round.'

They gave platitudes, asked questions: did she take clothes? Did she take her passport? Who spoke to her last? Has she done this before? Have you tried her mobile? Her bedroom, has it been tidied? Don't tidy it. Is there a recent photo? (Pretty) Don't panic. Leave it to us. Likely as not she'll be back in seventy-two hours, they usually are. Don't panic, people don't just disappear. One last thing: was there a boyfriend? A lad she was seeing?

No.

No way.

Not Faith.

They were wrong, the police. People do just disappear.

And don't panic? Wrong again.

Birmingham: grim place. Full of immigrants and idiots. Looks toxic at the best of times, let alone in the winter. Harry says his satnav had led them into the city through a labyrinth of ashen streets lined with Victorian terraces. The traffic's always slow there, and Harry says every now and then his windscreen wipers smoothed across the windscreen, revealing, through the grainy afternoon, ruptures of red from brake lights and traffic lights. Both say there'd been no conversation, no dialogue, and the air in the car would have felt thick-hot, crude and heavy. Maddie says she felt the throb of her heartbeat in her head, in her ears. Says she felt a creeping sense of something like sleep, like anaesthesia almost. She says she was still aware of Harry though, of his posture, too upright, too close to the wheel, too Harry. She says she tried not to look at him, tried not to notice the little golden hairs on the back of his left hand, the almost, but not quite, imperceptible ticking of his watch, his steady breathing – open mouthed, concentrating. All this, she tried to ignore.

She says it took a couple of seconds for her to register

the outside world, to work it out, to release herself from her own thoughts into the world she was in. Says it took time for her to work out that, outside, the thirtyish-year-old blonde wearing a black bra and panties and fishnet stockings, sitting in a bay window under the glow of a red light, was, in fact, a whore. And inside a similar window of the house next door, another, older, darker woman, sitting sidelong on, one hand stroking down a basque, part-baring a breast then motioning to someone, anyone, with her hands. Numbers, maybe. Amounts. Costs. Birmingham's Amsterdam. Maddie says she shuddered herself to a fuller consciousness, roused herself a little. Blinked and sat up. The area, she says, seemed busy with women. Huddled under an umbrella, two much younger girls stood at the corner. One, maybe Asian, wearing a short, bright orange skirt and pink stilettos, the other, mousy, smoking a cigarette and close enough to see she was chewing gum, stood shivering. Maddie remembers the concentrated synchronised dipping and ducking these girls performed, trying to catch the eye of drivers, trying to fix their gaze onto anyone – any chance. Maddie would have wanted to say something, to comment to Harry, but she kept quiet, turned her head to avoid those girls' eyes. But she wondered. She would have wondered. And then the traffic slowed to a stop again, and Maddie says she took another look. And there was a girl, a different one, standing alone on the greasy pavement, looking right at Maddie, right into her eyes. And Maddie says she felt it. A sort of unspecific connection. A flicker of something. She says the girl tilted her head, and on her neck, a series of purple oval bites stretched, stretching. Maddie says the girl looked like she never ate. Bones stuck out at awful angles through jeans and a grubby T-shirt. And her skin was crêpey, yellowish against the grey air. She might only have been thirteen, it was hard to tell. Rain had soaked her clothes so the thin material stuck to her, and – Maddie thought – she looked bizarre, pathetic, with her matted hair and tiny breasts and her obviously distended little belly. But Maddie remembers how this girl smiled. She smiled at Maddie, a big, wide, open smile. An honest smile. Like a welcome. Maddie remembers smiling back, or half-smiling. Half-smiling and breathing in, and almost smelling her, this girl. And then a man, a punter or a pimp, appeared from somewhere – one of those Victorian terraces maybe – and he seemed to call something to this girl, and she turned to him, and Maddie says she couldn't see the smile any more.

And then, quite suddenly, the traffic moved. Jerked forward. Harry would have driven forward with the flow, and Maddie ran her hand across her own flat belly and says she thought something about orders of bliss, or some such philosophical nonsense, and she felt her face crimp with the worry of it.

Harry spoke.

'Jesus,' he said, or something like it. And Maddie knew exactly what he meant.

Harry says he drove further north, towards the canal network and the smart waterside developments, the pseudo-weirdo mix of industrial chic warehouses. Old Birmingham's money-spinners, now full of nu-professionals: bankers, homosexuals, women.

But Jonathan didn't live there.

When Harry parked up, from a distance we might have been forgiven for believing he and Maddie were having a tiff. The car windows had steamed up a little so they – Maddie and Harry – were just vague silhouettes. Actually, they weren't talking. Harry was fiddling with the satnav, and Maddie, still holding Jonathan's business card, was gazing out towards the canal. It seemed like a couple of minutes before she got out of the car. Onlookers might have been struck by her paleness, or the clench of her jaw, or how small she seemed against the background mish-mash of geometric architecture. Without waiting for Harry, she seemed to set off, walking towards the towpath. And she walked quickly, as if she knew where she was going. And it was cold down by the canal, and there was a bitterness about the cold, as if all the chemicals and creatures and life and death in the water were conspiring against them. Against us all. It was as if the past and present were lost and found right there in the swirling air and ink-black water. And Maddie kept walking, away from the city, out, past the edges of disused factories, beyond the metropolitan blocks and buildings. Not far really. It isn't far before the city limits quite suddenly become an abandoned, unimproved no-man's land. Here, black weeds and oily mud line the water's edge, and that day, puddles of gradually icing mud had breached the earth to offer up dim reflections of overhead power lines. Alongside the towpath, the remains of a brick wall, graffitied with obscenities and pictures, and words, 'Have you seen him?' or something similar. But Maddie didn't notice. She says she didn't notice. For her, it was as if there was a faint smear of Vaseline on the lens, and she pushed her hands into her pockets, pulling the material tightly around her, so she looked even smaller. A strand of her hair had stuck itself to the dampness of her cheek, her lips, so her face looked broken as if something was misaligned. It was as if someone had picked away at the edges of this picture like a hangnail. Like they'd picked away at the pain of it. And then, quite suddenly, Maddie stopped. She stopped walking. She seemed to take a breath, as if to say something or sneeze maybe, but instead, she exhaled, slowly. The air released in a prolonged, complicated pattern. She'd obviously seen something, and was squinting through the weather at what she thought was a splash of garish colour on the water. Red, green, yellow. Imprecise brush strokes against a dirty canvas. And she walked on, almost ran, towards it as if, yes, as if she knew she was in the right place.

They are beautiful, narrowboats, in their own way. This one was beautiful. Sharply obtrusive, deliberately gaudy, but beautiful. Maddie counted the slatted windows: six. She said she saw the word painted in gold script on the side, then stood for a second, re-reading the address on the business card. Yes, *Viewfinder*, that's what it said. And bit by bit, she seemed to realise this was it. This was the place. This was the address on the business card. This was where Jonathan lived. This was where they'd find him. And with this realisation, came an incomprehensible slow-drip of relief. A slight loosening of something, as if all the bad memories, or something, had detached themselves and had begun flowing away from her. Poor Maddie. Of course, some detritus always gets stuck, snagged on lumps of weeds and metal and sorrow. Nothing ever really flows away, it just hides itself, ready, later on, to take us by surprise.

Without much hesitation, though, Maddie seemed to peer through a window for a second. She says she couldn't see much, so she hauled herself aboard. Two small doors, closed and held with an oversized brass padlock, led to the living quarters.

'What the fuck are you doing?' Harry had caught up, and his voice pounded at her. His shoes were muddy. She didn't answer.

'I've been calling your name. Why are you ignoring me?' He narrowed his eyes, as if he was looking at one of his year 7s who'd forgotten their homework.

Just looking at him, she says, made her feel suffocated, sick. And she closed her eyes and held the business card out to him. Harry took the card and seemed to take a long time to read it. So long, that he seemed to almost disappear into the mottled background. When he spoke, he just said, 'Right,' and nodded, and he seemed to age a thousand years, and all his vulnerability, all his fears would have risen to the surface of him. And, knowing Harry, all he was thinking was *Embrace me, Maddie. Why don't you embrace me?*

But Maddie didn't see it. She says she didn't see his thoughts any more. She was on the boat, tapping the door. 'Jonathan,' she was saying. 'Hello. Are you in there?' A little flock of grey birds noisily flapped into view, up and away, and Maddie started and took a breath as if to speak, but didn't. She was pulling at the door handle. She says she was as surprised as anyone when the brass padlock easily gave way, unclicked itself. Of course, it was never locked, but she didn't know that. So she opened the door. Easy. Harry was saying something, words barely discernible, but his intonation was violated by dread. When she stepped inside the boat, Maddie says she was instantly taken by the smell – earthy, warmish damp.

'Christ, come on, Maddie, we shouldn't even be here.' Harry's voice faded in like a bad recording, but Maddie waved the sound away. She'd expected it to feel bigger, this boat, expected it to have that magical feel of space you just wouldn't expect from the outside, but with them both in there, it felt small. Yes, that's how it felt, small and hopeless. She says she scanned the place, noticed a bizarrely small cast-iron wood-burner in the corner, a well-worn sofa, a little wooden table. She stepped further. Rooms led to rooms. Everything linked. Living room to kitchen to bedroom. She moved through the claustrophobic space, touching cushions, the table, an oven in the kitchen, a jar of coffee, open; a mug, half empty, a teaspoon with a whitish puddle of something on a yellow Formica work surface. Then the bedroom. The bed, made. A white duvet, white pillows. A white lamp. All white. This was simple stuff. She says she stooped down at the bedside table and pulled at the first drawer.

'Hey,' Harry said. 'What are you doing? Don't touch any-thing.'

Maddie sighed, but Harry persisted, apparently.

'Don't look through his things.'

'He's not here.' She says she was certain.

Harry says when she looked at him he noticed her make-up was smudged, and in the dimness she seemed to have the over-ly-calm look of a cancer patient or a starving child. Harry says he'd never thought of her like that before and he hesitated for a second or two. So she opened the drawer, and the scraping sound of wood against wood jolted them both. Harry says he couldn't help noticing the curve of Maddie's spine, how small she looked, how young, how thin her arms seemed. He watched her open the drawer, saw her fingers begin flicking, sorting through its contents, watched her pinched profile, mouth slightly open, seeming to hardly breathe. Against those white sheets she was fast becoming a silhouette, but Harry says he could taste her, taste her naivety, her guilt, and he re-members feeling his own heart beating like a spasm. Outside the air was turning brown but in there, in that boat, Harry was surrounded by white sheets, whiteness, and Maddie, still searching through that drawer. And it didn't feel cold in there to him. He says he felt warm, hot. He could feel sweat forming and trickling down his face, down his arms, collecting in his clenched palms. If we ask him, he doesn't seem to feel the need to explain why he did it – what he did next. But Maddie does. She says she heard him say something just as she found a folder at the bottom of the drawer and had caught her fingernail on a staple. She says she jumped up, swore and instantly stuck her bleeding finger into her mouth. With her other hand, she recovered the folder. There was something written on the front cover in small handwritten letters, but it was too dark to make it out, and when she flicked it open, she could feel the gloss of photographs. She says she felt tempted to flick on the lamp, but thought better of it. Instead, she closed the folder and would have turned to Harry, she would have turned to him and suggested they leave. Jonathan wasn't there. In some ways, it was as if he never existed. At least they knew now. They could talk, plan, decide what to do, how to handle it. How to handle themselves. But as she turned, as she tried to turn, she says she felt Harry's hands slip across her hips and felt his body closing in on her. She says his face felt sticky hot against the back of her neck and his hands seemed to clasp her too tightly across her waist. When she tried to release herself, to ease his hands off her, she says he seemed to grip her tighter still. She says it took her a second to work out what she thought might be happening, and in that second, Harry had leaned, pushed her sideways onto the bed and he was gripping her so tightly she thought she couldn't breathe. She couldn't speak. All hysteria squeezed into silence. No strength. No effort left. She needed faith, to show faith in him, to stop herself from falling apart, to prevent herself from unsticking. She says she could feel his mouth close to her ear, the warm saliva, hot breath on the tendons of her neck. He was still behind her, they must have looked like real lovers spooning, but somehow she says her hands were trapped then, beneath his arms or something, somehow her hands were useless, and she could feel his knees drawing up hard, too hard, and she could feel her dress straining and tearing a little, riding up over her thighs. She says she knew that a struggle would be pointless, that a struggle was mostly likely what he wanted, that most likely he wanted her to writhe and moan, to fight back, lash out, tear at him and his clothes, slap him, be a battle to win, a prize to be had. So she says she relaxed, let the darkness engulf her, just simplified it. And, almost immediately, she says she felt his fingers loosen and trace the contours of her hip and waist and breast, and felt his lips on the skin of her shoulder, and a slow pulsing from his chest against her spine. She remembers him lifting up her hand, the one with the bleeding finger, and she remembers feeling the warmth of the inside of his mouth around the tip of it. It was like she was letting him. But she remembers the water outside seemed to be reflected in dim complicated patterns on the far wall of the bedroom. She remembers wishing whatever would happen was over, wishing she was dead, thinking maybe she was dead and this was Hell, or Heaven. Then, just as everything was beginning to become imprecise to her, she says Harry moved his hand to her face – she felt his fingers spread out across her eyes and mouth, and tasted sourness.

'Do you feel guilty?' His voice, she says, was touching her skin. 'Do you?'

'Yes,' she said, but not straight away.

'You are guilty, you know,' he said, and she says she could smell his breath, metallic. She breathed him in.

'I am. I know I am,' she said, and her voice was somewhere else.

'But you'll always have me,' he said, and he moved his hand to rest heavily on her chest, like a restraint. She probably couldn't have moved even if she'd tried. 'No matter what, you'll always have me.' His voice was faltering, cracking, and Maddie felt a different warmth on her neck and knew it was tears.

She says she doesn't know how long they lay there, on Jonathan's bed, but when she felt his body cool and his grip, his embrace, loosen, she said, 'We have to go,' as if she was speaking to a child. 'We have to go,' again, and Harry released her. When she sat up, she says she looked at him, just a shadowy foetus-like figure lying on the white sheet.

'You know?' he whispered, not moving.

'Know what?' she said.

'What to do?'

Maddie says she fumbled around in the darkness, found the folder and picked it up. The back of her dress clung to her. She probably didn't realise she was trembling. She said, 'We have to go.'

Outside, a mist was starting to smother the towpath. Frost was settling and the air was painful. Harry missed his footing getting off the boat but didn't speak, and they could both hear the gruesome stillness of the water, could probably both feel intermittent surges of panic at the idea of threats lurking in the silt and the oil and the interconnectedness of the weeds. They walked quickly without speaking and say they could feel danger settled behind trees or bushes or walls; imagined danger waiting under bridges, behind lamp posts. Back towards the city, inside those warehouse apartments and around that car park: danger. Beneath the orange glow of street-lights, they could see the car, and for a moment let the panic subside, but then Harry says he saw it. It was definitely Harry who seemed to notice first. It was probably the glass on the floor near the tyres. Shards of glistening glass. Shards, not just splinters. Shards of broken glass splayed out on the tarmac. Zig-zag remains of the driver's window.

'Shit,' he said. 'Look at that. Somebody broke into the fucking car.'

They both looked. He, circling the vehicle, hands on hips; she, a step or two or three behind, hugging the folder under her chin, shivering in her torn dress.

'Look at that,' he said again, louder this time, directing his voice across the car park. A light pinged on in a second floor apartment and Maddie moved forward, ghost-like, expressionless, half-heartedly glancing at the damaged window. She shook her head.

'Let's just go,' she probably said, walking to the passenger side.

More lights illuminated the apartments, and voices or music or something leaked out into the night from somewhere. Harry's breath was coming in short white jabs as he kicked the glass away from the car with the toe of his shoe.

'Get in,' he said. Even from a distance, you could tell his teeth were gritted.

And Maddie got in.

Harry slammed his door, started the engine and drove off fast without seeming to look. That's the thing about anger, it clouds things, makes us temporarily blind. Only temporarily. But still, it was odd. Odd that they didn't notice straight away. In fact, Maddie says it was a while, maybe ten or even fifteen minutes later that she realised. She didn't say anything, but she wondered what had been taken from the car. The satnav was still there – strangely – and when she reached across to the back seat for the blanket, she realised what had gone, what was missing. It was the school blazer, of course, the one with the ropes and a lion on the pocket. It was gone.

It's these moments when we have to wish we'd been there. According to Maddie, she was just processing this information, trying to piece together what might have happened, handicapped by freezing cold and all sorts of misalignments in her head, when Harry stopped the car at a set of traffic lights on the Hagley Road. Maddie was wondering whether she'd imagined it. Who, after all, would break into a car, steal a school blazer and leave a satnav? The folder felt heavy against her chest and she couldn't work out what had possessed her to bring it with her. Some crazy memento maybe. Curiosity. It killed the cat. Nothing was making sense to her. Nothing. Her head was spinning. She says she felt a bit sick. Sharp gritty cold was blowing in through the broken window but she says she'd stopped shivering. The lights changed to green and the cars ahead moved. But Harry didn't move. Maddie says she could hear the throb of the engine and the hissing of weather outside. She says she glanced sideways at Harry, and when she saw him staring blankly forward, says she felt tempted to escape. And she probably would have. She could have just opened the car door and escaped. Left him to it. Walked away, or got a taxi or something, anything. She should have. That's the moment she should have left him. But Harry spoke, he said, 'It was wrong,' and then, according to Maddie, he looked at her. A car horn interrupted but she says he carried on as if he hadn't heard, 'All wrong.'

'Harry, just drive.' She would have sounded impatient and turned her face away.

'No, hear me out, I have to tell you.' She says he was still looking at her, a haze of green light cast over the side of his face. 'It's important.'

'It's not important now. This is mad. Drive, please, Harry.'

'I did something.'

'I know, I know, I know . . .'

'You don't know.'

More car horns. Some shouting.

'This isn't the place. Not here.'

'You don't know. That's why I have to tell you. I have to tell you.'

'Christ, Harry, please. What we did was terrible. We're both guilty, we are, but we can't talk about it here . . .'

'That's not it. No, not that.' Harry probably thumped the steering wheel. Maddie says she turned to him and red light faded across their faces and settled in the lines around Harry's eyes. She says she tried to look at him, but couldn't.

'I'm a fucking idiot. I am. I've ruined everything. It's all ruined,' he said.

Behind them a buzz of anger and irritation threatened, and both of them could feel the metabolic rate of the city and the drivers and the place they'd left behind. Maddie would have turned her face and looked out of the window. The cold air might have made her nose run but she wouldn't have wiped it away. She says she knew that a struggle was mostly likely what he wanted, that most likely he wanted her to writhe and moan, to fight back, lash out, tear at him and his clothes, slap him, be a battle to win, a prize to be had. So she says she relaxed, let the darkness engulf her. She needed to have faith, and she knew it. When the lights changed, Harry drove on.

Faith. It was raining when she got home. She was wet. Dripping. Somewhere along the line, she'd lost her blazer. Left it somewhere. She went straight to her room. It was dark and she wasn't sure of the time. She knew school had been in touch, they're hot on absence, especially with good kids like her. Good school. Nice uniform. Blazers with emblems. Ropes and a lion. She was cold. Her room, it looked like the beginning of a nightmare sequence in a Stanley Kubrick film: pretty boy posters plastered the walls, but the contents of her Critical Thinking folder were strewn across her duvet, and there was a picture on the front of the Sixth Form prospectus of a girl in a white coat. She would have got into the Sixth Form. She would. Easy.

She'd have thought about writing a note, maybe she'd have torn a page from her diary, might have written 'I'm sorry' but perhaps her gel pen ran out, or something. Maybe she realised she was scared. Maybe it was her unnatural obsession with love and death – they all seem to have that these days.

That doesn't make it any easier though.

We can guess she must have felt sickish and ugly. She most likely felt empty. She might have thought about eating but decided not to. She didn't know it, but it was only about

4pm when she took a handful of paracetamol, put them in her mouth, gagged at the bitterness and spat them back up onto the floor. There's still a little patch of fading white on her bedroom carpet.

She cried then. For a long time.

Probably.

Maddie's hands were cold. She says she'd almost forgotten she was still holding the folder. Rain or sleet had battered her fingers and the side of her face, coming in sideways from Harry's broken window. He wasn't protecting her, or so it seemed. His body, that is, it wasn't protecting her. She says the rain, or whatever it was, seemed to go right through his head and neck and stiffened jaw, and seemed to sharpen, then bite into her skin. And her lips, she says they ached from pursing them. She would have been grateful for the darkness of that car, grateful for the concentration required of Harry to safely navigate the dual carriageway and the several quirky, back-to-front Black Country roundabouts, back to the dimly lit street where they kind of lived.

When he parked up outside their house, Harry didn't speak, but sat and seemed to be waiting. Maddie says she thought she saw a trail of self pity just on the edge of her sight – a small snail trail of self indulgence down his cheek, down his lips, down his chin, and thought he was breathing like he might be about to say something. So she moved quickly. She says that's what she did. She says she rushed, out of his car, into the bitter street, slipping a bit and almost falling on the greasy tarmac, steadying herself on the bonnet of her own car, parked up where she'd left it. And the wind, it felt like a gust of hatred to her. And then her keys, perhaps they didn't seem to fit the lock of the front door. She had a bunch, and maybe none of them seemed to fit, and let's say she'd bitten the skin around her fingernails, so there would have been hard white specks and a lump of cold redness at the tip of her fingers. And imagine her fingers. Imagine they wouldn't work. They just wouldn't work. So it would have been Harry who, suddenly appearing behind her, would have slipped his key into the lock, maybe rested his hand on her arm. And Maddie could get into her own house.

They'd left the light on in the kitchen, and Maddie says it was buzzing like it might give up at any moment. She says she dropped the folder on the kitchen table, and watched her breath escape. She says she felt Harry touch the sleeve of her jacket and heard him say something about the cold, saw him flick the central heating switch and heard the kitchen radiator click a couple of times. She says a grey cobweb fluttered in the corner of the ceiling and down a wall, and there was a damp patch she hadn't noticed before. Harry, she says, was looking right at her, saying something. She'd noticed there was a little pile of breadcrumbs or fluff or grit or something on the floor, and the knife was still there, on the floor, near his feet. The handle of the kitchen cupboard behind him looked odd, loose maybe, and the door didn't close properly, and beneath the cupboard, in that dim light, the work surface where he was leaning, with its tea stains and dirty mugs and odd bits and pieces, reminded her of her student days.

And Harry was still talking.

She says she thought how earnest he looked. Maybe he'd lost weight recently. And he was hawkishly talking. On and on and on. She says she wondered why he hadn't fixed that kitchen cupboard door. It really did look odd. She hates those kitchen cupboards. Always has. Pretend wood. Pretend farmhouse kitchen. Cheap, brassy handles, old and sticky now, prone to falling off and clanking onto the hard stone floor. They'd said they would renovate it four years ago, this kitchen, when they moved in. That was their plan, to replace this kitchen.

Maddie would have shuddered. She hates that kitchen. Everything looks brown. Too brown.

Harry stepped back sideways and crunched that grit or those breadcrumbs or whatever it was. She would have heard that, looked at the floor and wondered what possessed the previous owners to choose stone slabs. Always cold. Always. She says she wished they'd ripped it all out years ago, but, according to Maddie, Harry never received that promotion he'd apparently been promised, and then there was the property slump and people stopped moving home, so no bonuses for her. So that was that. Brown kitchen. And she hated the brown of it.

Harry, leaning against the work surface still, talking, still, ran his hand through his hair a couple of times, shoving it off his hawk face, pushing the wet strands of brown back. Smoothing it and smoothing it. All brown and smooth. And Maddie, she says she watched his lips moving. Dry lips, wintered, frilled with dry skin. Only a couple of hours ago, those lips had been on her neck, on the skin of the back of her neck. She says she felt the prickle of a kind of heat on her throat, her chin, her cheeks, her forehead, and then Harry was saying, 'I don't go along with that,' and he was shaking his head, and Maddie thought how close together his eyes were. She says she'd never noticed that before. How beady and brown they were, and too close together.

She didn't blame herself for anything, usually, Maddie didn't. And as she watched Harry going on and on – not listening to his words, just watching him going on and on – she would have let herself think about the others, about Jonathan. She would have let herself think of all the other times, all the other ways. She likes men. Other men, that is. If she didn't know it before, she would have realised it then, and as she watched Harry's face, Harry's mouth, Harry's darting brown eyes and wet brown hair, she came to thinking it would be down to her to sort this mess out.

'You're smiling,' she heard him say.

'What?' she said.

'Smiling.' And his relief, the sound of it, would have made everything seem a shade browner to Maddie then.

And then he probably smiled one of his smiles at her.

Maddie says she took a swift breath in and caught a smell of something. Caught a smell of herself. A smell of Harry on her. And she probably swallowed hard, looked away.

'Shut up. Just shut up, why don't you?' she said.

When Harry swept past her, into the hall and away from her, he must have caught that smell. Something sour, warmish, familiar, catfoodish. He probably wasn't smiling any more as he bounded upstairs. And Maddie remained in the kitchen, looking at the mess, and the bits of grit, and the knife on the floor.

It's easy to disappear someone. It is, really. Especially someone who is already half invisible – better yet if they're also broken. If you just have faith. Some people don't, and need to be taught how to have it. Faith, that is. Schoolgirls need to be taught how to have faith. Most of them are too interested in documenting their lives than actually living it. Social networking. That's a joke. Most are more interested in pretending to be celebrities or someone they're not on Facebook than being themselves. They get influenced.

See, that was Faith's big downfall.

But it's OK.

She went missing on a Monday.

Imagine: Harry sleeping on the sofa that night. A periodic flutter of orange light from outside rippling across his face and his hands and his feet. Imagine him, foetal, chilly, hoping that Maddie would come downstairs and ask him to go to bed, with her. Imagine he does get some sleep, just a little, and his dreams are filled with hearts and flowers, and when he jolts himself awake, as if he'd been plunged into ice-cold water, he re-runs his conversation with Maddie in the kitchen. Re-runs his confession, the justification, edits out the clichés, the mention of the 'big mistake', the 'just a fling', the 'it'll never happen again'. His parting shot, though, the bit about loving Maddie more than he could ever love a fourteen-year-old girl, the bit about how most couples couldn't cope with this, the bit where he said 'I don't go along with that.' That bit would stay. Especially now, after Jonathan. Imagine how he re-runs it all in his head, not quite sure if she was listening or not. And imagine Harry, hearing Maddie padding about upstairs, most, but not all of the night. Little footsteps, like a child's footsteps. Tracking them, her footsteps, with his brown eyes across the ceiling. Occasionally maybe he'd hear her cough, or seem to cough, and then the footsteps might stop. Imagine him wishing he had the guts to go upstairs, hold her, soothe her, stroke her worries away. Like he used to. Maybe then he'd drift off into a shallow sleep. Very shallow. But the milkman, clinking bottles and growling off down the road like some lion or other would have woken him completely awake. So, imagine, Harry, spiky-haired and blotchy eyed, joints aching, needing the bathroom, creeping upstairs – not needing a light, even in the darkness of the very early morning. He knows every fibre of the carpet, every graze against his socks. Imagine him noticing the bedroom door slightly, very slightly ajar. Imagine him tiptoeing across the landing, pushing the door gently, gently – he knows it creaks if you push too hard. Imagine him seeing Maddie lying on the bed, facing the window. Imagine: she hasn't closed the curtains so she's bathed in this bluishness, and he can see her mouth is slightly open, and if he couldn't hear the catch of each breath in her throat, he might believe she's dead. He looks at the way her hair has fallen sideways across her shoulder, across her chest, resting in the crushed skin between her small breasts. She's still wearing her dress and the sleeves have crumpled down so he can see the smoothness of her shoulder and he notices the way the material clings to her waist and the curve of her hip. And he can see her thighs and her calves, and her feet look poised, like a ballerina, and small.

She jumps – more like a twitch – and swallows a couple of times, and Harry retreats a little, but her dress rides up, just a little, and her thighs seem to glisten in that bluish light. To Harry, they do. He's tempted, of course – painfully so. But he steps quietly away, probably feeling good about himself, noble, and lets the door return to its semi-closed state as he creeps to the bathroom without even noticing the way Maddie is clutching onto that folder.

The shower is hot, and the hot stings at first just make Harry feel colder. When he closes his eyes, he sees Maddie. Maddie's mouth – Maddie's skin, hears her breath. He wishes, wishes, wishes, and can't seem to help thinking about that moment – more than a moment – they had on that canal boat. Jonathan's canal boat. He knows that's the man she wants him to be. He felt it then, and he can feel it now. Feels it more surely than ever. He suddenly feels alive. There's a fuzzy buzz inside his head. He can't forget that moment they had on Jonathan's white sheets. The feel of her breasts and the skin of her neck, the taste of her. He feels his jaw clenching, and without even drying off, without even dressing, without even turning off the shower, he pads out of the bathroom, across the landing and into the bedroom. Their bedroom. As he pushes open the door, he's sure. He feels strong. He wants to push away the hair from her face, from her shoulders, strip away the doubt, make her see how he feels. He is sure. This is how she wants him to be. And if he has it wrong, it doesn't matter to him. He'll make her see how it should be. He will. Maybe she'll see him, see his wet skin, smell the shampoo in his hair. Maybe she'll be reluctant at first, but any objection will only be for show. A temporary no. And anyway, he's stronger than her. Physically stronger. And as he walks into their bedroom, fast, feeling the carpet's fibres between his toes, and the sinews of his knees and hips, his naked skin tingling against the chill of the room, he's blinded for a couple of seconds into seeing her lying there, mouth slightly open, breasts almost exposed, thighs smooth. And he sits on their bed and blinks. And the blue light from outside is hardening into day.

Imagine Harry's face as he double-blinks to reality and runs his damp hand across the contours of the duvet and ruffled pillows. He might imagine he can make out the shape of Maddie's body, lying sideways on the bed. He might imagine he can still feel her heat or smell her body or her breath. And he might be right. But her dress is hanging over the back of a chair like it's been spilt there, and downstairs, the front door is slamming. Maddie's wearing trousers and boots.

She's driving to work today.

And she's taking no chances – she's taking that folder with her.

It's hard to make someone good. Harder than you'd think. Faith, for instance. She went to church, prayed, sang hymns, kissed the crucifix. It's like this, see: you can show someone the way, give them every reason, but as for making them good, that's hard. In the end, you have to take responsibility, whatever the consequences. And whatever people say about

Maddie Harper, however they describe her, 'good' she is not.

That day, she says she arrived at work early, very early. Too early to work. Nobody buys houses at 6.30am. But that wasn't why she was at work.

She says she'd let herself into the shop-front office, managed somehow to press in the number of the alarm with dead fingers and placed the folder, the one she'd taken from Jonathan's boat, on her desk. It didn't look out of place amongst the other buff-coloured folders and, just for a second, she stood and looked at it. The cold would have made her nose run, but maybe she couldn't feel it. A couple of cars passed by outside. The day was already starting. She might have felt a bit exposed, standing under the down-lighters, surrounded by pictures of other people's unwanted property, and the heating would have just clicked on, so a warmish breeze of air might have ruffled her hair a little. That's probably why she sat down, gently – obviously – behind her desk, behind her computer, like no-one would be able to see her. The feeling was most likely starting to come back into her fingers, and, probably, without thinking, she picked at the hardened skin near her thumb nail. With the other hand, she flicked open the folder, then spread the four photographs out on her desk. Black and white images. Pictures. That's how well I know Maddie, see. That's how well I know her. Of all the things she could have found on that boat, I knew it would be this. Even from across the street, looking into that dimly lit shop front with its pictures of repossessions and houses, sold, dangling on string in the window, you could just see her picking at her thumb, and you could see she was thinking 'I don't know you at all, do I?' as she examined those four photographs.

And after a while you could see her jaw jutting, and see she was nibbling and picking away at that skin on her fingers, still examining each photograph in turn like she was shortsighted. And it's always been this about her, this vulnerability, that gives hope, that gives faith.

Harry says he'd thought about calling in sick. His Mondays were usually filled with depression and failure, but this weekend he hadn't marked any books, hadn't prepared any lessons, and there was the department meeting to attend after school. He says he'd thought about taking the day off, maybe a few days, buying Maddie some flowers, maybe booking a table somewhere for dinner. They'd had a stressful time. When he'd heard her leave that morning, he says he'd raced downstairs, and only when he was about to open the front door to call her back, realised his nakedness and thought about the neighbours – Steve or Phil or whoever it was next door. This is what he says, anyway. Still naked, he says, he returned to their bedroom, fiddled in his jacket pocket, fished out his phone amongst the loose change, and scrolled through his contacts, rotating his thumb through name after name, and then stopping it, like some 21st century wheel of fortune on 'F', looking for Falborough High School Sickline, letting the soft skin of the tip of his thumb rub the screen, and then maybe seeing the school's details and stopping. We can only imagine Harry standing naked, gawping, his face a mask of blurred yellow from the glow of his phone. We can only imagine him hesitating – there would have to be a hesitation – then selecting a number, holding the phone to his ear – still damp with shampoo – and waiting, initially, with forced patience, and hesitating again before reaching for a couple of tissues from Maddie's bedside table. And as he listened, the ring tone changed to answerphone, and we can imagine his face settling into that lazy look of memory and greed, and we might imagine him, with his free hand, stroking the line of dark hair from his navel downwards.

It wasn't school he was calling.

Not that morning.

If you check his phone, you'll see he called her number four times that morning. The answerphone message is shortish, childish: 'Hey,' it says, 'you've reached Faith's phone, but I'm not around just now, sorry. I'm probably listening to music, or perhaps even studying, ha, ha! But seriously, call me back later. Kisses.'

He probably thought she was still in bed, asleep, but as he slipped his phone back into his jacket pocket, he ought to have been wondering if he should have called her at all.

Just before he left for work, just as he was adjusting his tie, he must have noticed the used tissues on the bedroom floor. He must have wondered what was best, he might have left them – Maddie wouldn't have cared, and he would have known that. But he scooped them up, those tissues, and says he pushed them into his jacket pocket. He must have thought it was for the best.

And later, school. The air in his classroom would have battered him even before he'd begun his day. After a weekend, especially after a weekend, with locked and bolted windows and doors, it was as though all the particles of the week before had settled and ripened and strengthened and attacked him as he walked in.

Although it would have been quite early when he arrived, he says there were a couple of pupils hanging around in the corridor, eating crisps and swigging energy drinks. Naughty kids who'd been mini-bussed in from the council estate across town; special needs kids who, in Harry's opinion, were anything but special.

'Morning, girls,' he said, as he passed them, on his way to the photocopier.

'Fuck off,' he thought one of them said, though he wasn't

sure. When he looked back he says he noticed the outline of a black bra beneath her white school shirt.

He says he had to wait for the photocopier to warm up, and as he did, felt the chill of school spread over him, says he shoved his hand into his jacket pocket, let the tips of his fingers play with the tissue, and absent-mindedly stroked it.

'Mr Logue?' He says he heard the Principal's voice and turned. 'You're an early bird.'

Imagine Harry pushing the button on the photocopier and twisting his fingers into the centre of his palm.

'Yes.' His laugh would have been nervous. 'Things to do.'

And who knows what Harry would have thought about as duplicated pages clicked into view.

So the day began, for Harry.

And his first lesson: year 10, so he says. They would have arrived in dribs and drabs, topping up his classroom with a wet-animal smell. They would have lolled about on their plastic chairs, fiddling with their phones or shouting something at someone furthest away. Every one of them would have ignored him. Harry might have felt his shoulders drooping, and the seconds ticking by. He remembers an argument between two girls was only interrupted by a mobile phone's ringtone. Harry said, 'Right, guys,' and he says they all still ignored him.

Two girls at the back of the class laughed simultaneously, so Harry says. He says he noticed one of them was the girl with the black bra.

'No phones, guys, you know the rules.' He says he could barely be heard above the rabble.

'Guys,' he said, a little louder, 'phones away now, please.'

The two girls laughed again, and the phone rang again, and the talk was loud, like a party, he says.

'Let's make a start,' Harry said, picking up a pile of folders from his desk, and as he looked round the class, he says he felt his eyelid twitch.

'Guys,' he said, and he says he was shouting a little.

'Guys,' the girl with the black bra said, and shrieked another laugh.

From Harry's viewpoint at the front of the class, they all looked like aliens. The girls, with their lip-gloss and too much eyeliner, and the boys, already with scratched tattoos on arms that would probably never lift anything any heavier than a tray of fast food across a counter. And as they, these kids, sat mostly sideways, ululating at each other, Harry says he felt his eyes narrow and the corners of his mouth draw down and back.

'We'll make a start now,' he said, and he says he was walking down, between the desks, between the conversations and the disagreements, towards the back of the room.

'Alicia,' he said, handing the girl with the black bra the pile of folders, 'give these out, would you please?'

Another shriek of laughter, he says.

'What?' the girl said, not taking the folders.

'Could you give these folders out, please?' Harry said, and he says he noticed she was chewing something. Her pink, glittery lips were overfilled, animated.

'What did you call me?' The girl, he remembers, had a loud voice and a big face, and she'd stopped laughing. Somewhere, not too many generations ago, some inbreeding must have taken place, and the focus of those eyes was slightly off – Harry says he noticed this – but it was her voice the class was interested in, and she would have known that.

'What did you call me?' she said again, louder this time. 'What name?'

Harry says one of the boys sniggered and clapped his hand over his mouth, looking wildly about, happy to attract anyone's attention. Harry says he could see him out of the corner of his eye. And the girl stood up, not tall, and Harry says he saw her draw back her top lip, so the glimmer of pink lip-gloss on her front tooth was caught by the classroom's fluorescent light.

'It's A-lee-sha,' she said, and Harry says he noticed her hands were on her hips.

And the class was silent now, and still.

Harry remembers clearly how he narrowed his eyes against the chill from her, let his gaze flick down at the shadow beneath her shirt.

'Right,' he said, and on the very edge of his nerves, he says he felt a tingle. 'Would you mind giving these folders out, please.'

The girl didn't move, except for her lips. Harry's eyes rested on them, and he says it was as if she knew it, and she parted them slowly, as if she might say something – protest, or something. Harry would have liked that. He says he knew that most of the class was watching, resentfully keen to see which one, pupil or teacher, would take control. And Harry knew it was all about control here. He says he let his eyes flicker across the girl's face, and rest on her lips, still parted. He says it was like he couldn't really help it.

'Is that lipstick you're wearing?' he said, quite quietly.

Except for an electrical hum, the class would have been silent now.

The girl's cheeks pricked with colour, but, according to Harry, she said nothing. Harry says he stepped forward, closer to her, as if he was examining a laboratory specimen, and with his free hand, says he reached into his jacket pocket, let his fingers close round the tissue.

'Make-up isn't allowed, you know that,' he said.

The girl's face hardened, Harry says she pursed her lips.

'Here,' he said. 'Wipe it off.'

He thought only she could possibly hear. And he says he pulled the tissue from his pocket and held it out in the palm of his hand, like a gift.

She might have refused. She could have. But Harry, he says he didn't move, his face was still. It was all about control. But she hesitated. Harry says he saw the muscles of her forehead ripple a little, tighten, and then sag, and, it seemed, quite suddenly, she snatched the tissue from his hand, and in one movement, wiped the paper across her lips. Harry says he heard the squeak of air against her skin, and watched the glistening smear settle across her cheek. He says she blinked a couple of times, maybe more, and slowly, very slowly, he saw the pink tip of her tongue flick to the corner of her mouth, and then he says her features seemed to recede, like she wanted to escape. It all seemed involuntary, natural. To Harry, she didn't look like a child any more. To Harry, it looked like her mind was racing and the little muscles of her jaw seemed to spasm. She wasn't looking at him though, Harry says she was looking at the tissue in her hand. She was looking like she was trying to work something out – a complicated mathematical thing, perhaps. Harry says he felt his shoulders straighten and his lips stretch. He could see he had control. He remembers taking a long breath in through his mouth, feeling his lips drying. And right on the very, very edge of his thoughts were white sheets, white walls.

'Good girl.' He says he whispered it, and leaned forward. 'Alicia.'

It's possible that her chin was trembling, just a little, as she raised her eyes to his.

And the quiet in the room was not interrupted, except for the push of that hum, electrical, maybe.

It could have stayed like that, suspended, for a while, and it might have done but Harry says he saw the girl's eyes change shape and direction and saw the ice in them, and in their reflection, behind him, the classroom door swung open, and he says cold air and the smell of gravy spoilt it.

'Mr Logue, may I have a word?' It was the Principal, in the classroom, at the front, scanning the room. Harry would have looked one last time at the girl's face with its tightening sliver of paleness, would have taken the tissue from her clammy fingers.

'Certainly,' he said. And though he can't be sure, he thinks he saw her shudder.

Still scanning the room, the Principal said, 'There's a message for you in Reception, a phone call. It sounded important, apparently. I'll cover for you here.'

And as Harry's walk turned into a sprint through the school corridors, he pressed that sticky tissue deep into his jacket pocket.

Even now there are black marks on the canal towpath. Even today, if we look, we'll see them etched into the concrete like scars. It's as if the driver might have changed her mind at the last moment and braked hard before the car slid into the water. It might have just been the slurry of ice that made her lose a bit of control.

That's not what she says though.

She doesn't lose control, Maddie doesn't.

Maddie says she doesn't lose control.

She says she'd decided by the time she arrived at work exactly what she was going to do. She says she'd put on her trousers and boots – warm clothes – and gone into work early. She says she'd sorted a few things out and made up some story in an email to her boss about needing to nip back home. Her car was beginning to ice up white and she sat inside it with the heater blasting until she could see out. She didn't shiver. Not once. So she says. But she says her ears hurt and her fingers were dead, clamped, without gloves, round the steering wheel.

She says the thought had started to come to her easily that morning. She had been woken, still dressed on the bed, by the sound of water. The room smelt sour to her, like someone had left their dirty washing in a corner for a while. As her eyes focused through the open curtains, she says she started to see clearly what she must do. Outside, the place looked submerged beneath a dirty mist. The row of terraced houses that backed onto theirs still slept, and there in the distance, just on the horizon beyond the ring-road and away, was the pointy outline of the church spire. Maddie would have blinked away the crusts of sleep, and when she rubbed her eyes, she might have been able to feel the skin trying to twitch. But in her head, it all seemed to be getting clearer.

Before leaving that morning, she says she hesitated outside the bathroom door. She says she could smell wet flannels or something, and even when she went downstairs, she could virtually taste Harry's breath, hear him thinking. So she left the house quite quickly. Escaped. It wasn't quite light enough for her to see she'd put her coat on inside out. But, of course, she had the folder. She was carrying it tightly against her chest, so the knuckles of her hand faded blue-white against the cold.

A little later, sitting in her car, waiting for the ice to clear, she might have had a moment of doubt, but it was too late then. Or so she thought. And, of course, she needed to keep a tight grip, Maddie did, she needed to keep a tight hold, a control.

Harry doesn't remember much of the conversation he had on the school's telephone, except that the official's voice was local, matter-of-fact. He didn't hear the girl's voice – Aleesha

– calling something at him out of the window as he ran to his car, didn't see the Principal's pursed lips and squinty eyes. And the journey to the hospital is still a tepid blur. He remembers having to spend twenty minutes or so looking for a parking space though; remembers swearing at various vehicles and pedestrians, and eventually parking his car half-on and half-off a grass verge round the corner from A&E.

And he says he felt like Maddie had pushed him too far this time.

He remembers breaking into a sprint, partly to avoid being snowed on. He remembers, inside, the building smelt of Starbucks. Three rows of plastic chairs, empty, were hemmed in by various large vending machines. There are other things he remembers too, like the Chinese woman behind the sweeping circular counter who didn't seem to notice him at first, but as he approached her, seemed to pick up a phone and have a whispered conversation. Harry says he felt a tightening around his chest and neck, a squeezing of his heart, noticed the irregular jerking of his tie against the buttons of his shirt. He says he fought the sudden urge to turn and run, says he knew it was up to him to keep hold of the situation now.

'Hi.' He would have tried to sound normal. 'You've called me about Madeleine Harper.'

The Chinese woman, he noticed, was wearing false eyelashes, long and black against her pale skin. And with her very small, scaled-down body, she was doll-like, hardly a woman at all. Exquisite. And Harry looked. And as he looked, he felt his heart settle – he did – and he smoothed his tie down with a steady hand and said, 'I think you said she's had an accident.' And he felt himself smile then, and the Chinese woman smiled back. Tiny white teeth and glossy lips. Harry noticed them. He noticed her slender white neck, and the smooth skin of her arms, and the speed with which her acrylic finger nails tapped the keyboard. He remembers noticing all of this and wondering if anything about her was real. Yet just behind that little woman, on the wall behind her, the 'Missing Persons' and the 'Have you seen?' stared at him from a community notice board.

And he didn't see.

He didn't see it.

He just wasn't looking.

They had left Maddie in a room by herself. It was all white walls and hard white sheets. Someone had taken her trousers and boots and her inside-out coat, and replaced them with a starchy white surgical gown. The first thing Maddie says she noticed when she woke up was how hard the bed was, and the second thing was her finger-nails – filthy with green blackness. She says she hadn't expected that. She sat herself up, so she'll tell us, and felt her chest, heavy. She rattled a cough, heaving up a little puddle of sizzling spittle, and says she tasted the metallic grease of her own blood. When she rubbed her belly, it felt flat, empty, and it hurt. And her face hurt. This is what she says.

Harry entered the room so quietly, she says she didn't hear him. The first she knew of him being there was feeling the bed tilt with his weight, feeling the sheets tighten around her body.

'Maddie,' he was whispering. 'Stop crying.'

She remembers feeling the edge of his finger or thumb across her cheek. She remembers wishing he'd stop talking. She remembers thinking how true it must be that your life flashes in front of you at the moment before death. And her life had flashed in front of her. And as she lay in that bed, she says she was thinking how pathetic, how meaningless her stupid life was, how many mistakes she'd made. She was wondering what she'd actually achieved in her life. She says it was only then that it occurred to her, only then that she realised how much time she'd wasted. She'd wasted her time at university, screwed up and screwed around, settled on Harry and a pointless job in a soulless town. She says she realised then she'd made the wrong choice. She says it only came to her there and then, in that hospital room. She says she wondered exactly what she'd ever done right.

'What have I done?' she said, and it hurt her to speak.

And she remembers Harry standing up, quickly.

'What have you done?'

She says he sounded odd; at least, she thought he did.

'You tell me what you've done, if you can explain it.'

'No, no,' she said and she remembers a pain, she remembers her head was pounding. 'No, I didn't mean that . . .'

'You didn't mean *what*?' And Harry was back down on the bed again, pinning her beneath the sheets, one hand either side of her. 'You didn't mean to drive your car into the fucking canal?'

She says she could feel his thumbs scratching swift, dangerous arcs on the sheets. His face was close enough to kiss.

'What were you fucking thinking?' And she says she flinched his breath away, turned her head to the side. 'And don't you dare tell me you wanted to top yourself.'

'I didn't.' She says she twisted herself loose and flinched against the pains in her chest and her arms and her skin. 'I didn't want that. I'm not suicidal, for god's sake.'

'No.' Harry, he seized the moment and she says she felt him squeezing her tight beneath the sheets. 'No, you're not suicidal – no, you're not mad, are you? Oh no. You're just a fuck-up, Maddie.'

And he let her go quite unexpectedly, let go of her. She says it was like he thought he had control of her. And she says she watched his face tighten into one of his smiles. And she says, beneath those tight sheets, she says she felt her flesh creep.

She brought me things. Maddie did. Maddie brought me things. That time, she brought me soup. After a while, we talked. Something about the weather or something. She had a camera – she always had a camera, because of her job. A camera or a phone. She seemed to me to talk in images, or metaphors. And she was starting to look like she never ate. Bones stuck out through her clothes. Poking hips and shoulder blades. And her skin – it could have just been the light – but it seemed yellowish. She might have been fourteen or forty.

Something was on her mind that time. Some problem or other. Would I listen? I wasn't busy, hadn't had any work in months, so I said yeah, of course, whatever. She looked sort of pleased, though I should have known she would always be trouble then. I looked around my studio – well, I say studio, it's a cellar really, but I call it a studio. It's perfect for my purposes, now, of course, but then, well, then it was sad with unfinished projects, cogs and wheels of work, scattered about like starving children, not quite dead yet, but dying, nonetheless. The soup revived me a little and when she finished talking, I stood up, stretched. I wished for a window I could see out of. I imagined a purplish sunset. She came over to me and snaked her arms round my waist, ran her fingers up my spine. The top of her head rubbed against the stubble on my chin. She smelt a bit like oil or something synthetic, and cold.

'Let's do it, now,' she said, and the words were warm against my chest. I looked down at almost the exact same time she turned her face up to mine, and she moved her lips up to my neck. Not quite a kiss.

'Let's do it now,' she said again, and I can still remember the taste of her breath. Like metal.

Then she was holding my hands and walking backwards, slow motion. When I looked, I saw she wasn't wearing any shoes. I didn't remember seeing her take her shoes off. She must have sensed my confusion and put her finger to her lips, saying 'Ssshhh,' like she was talking two-year-old, but not like a mother would. When she started unbuttoning her blouse, I said, 'Look, it's been a while, and, you know, I'm not alone. We should be careful.' But by that time her blouse was on the floor and her face was set. I could see she wouldn't handle a refusal, and after what she'd told me, it didn't seem to be an option.

And she was beautiful, kind of.

At that time, in that circumstance, you would have thought the same. We'd have felt exactly the same.

'Come here,' she said, and the pupils of her eyes had disappeared, and she lay down sideways. I didn't even notice the cold any more as I kicked off my own shoes, peeled off my T-shirt, let her do the rest. All the time looking at her, watching every bit of her – the way the skin on her neck strained, the way her lips were always parted, even when I kissed them. And her eyes, mostly closed. Mostly. Like she wasn't sure she needed to see my heart tearing in two.

And afterwards, she slept, or seemed to sleep, and – you'd have done the same, you'd have wanted to capture the moment, capture a memory – I reached over to where her camera was. And it was easy. Just clicks in the dark: a close-up of the crook of her neck, the angle of her collar bone, the pull of skin over her ribs, her hard concave belly, the way she lay with her arms by her sides and her hands clasped like a boxer, and her face twisted away.

Still beautiful though, more than ever.

To me, anyway, then.

I needed to remember that. It was important.

I thought about getting dressed. Pulled my jeans on. Pulled them off again.

I slept then, I don't know how long for, but she was gone by the time I woke up. A tangled sheet was still warm, and dust motes fizzed as I rubbed my hand across it, feeling for her body. I sat up and my head ached. I needed water. She must have rinsed her hands or face before she went, there was still a film of something oily lining the little sink in the corner. I rubbed the tips of my fingers round the basin, felt the scum collect under my finger-nails. When I breathed in the smell of it, put my finger-tips under my nose, closed my eyes and breathed in, it was her I could smell. I was close to her again.

It was a while before I noticed, I don't know how long exactly, but she'd left it on the desk. There was a lot of junk mail and some bits and pieces, but in amongst the screwdrivers and straps was a different type of movement. She'd written it on a scrap of tissue paper: 'You probably won't see me again. Thanks. Sorry.' I had to read it a couple of times. Trying to connect the words. Feeling my hands shaking. I put the note back on the desk. Placed it right back where I'd found it. I could see, when I looked, she'd found all her clothes, her bag, her bits and pieces.

I nodded, but only to myself.

My clothes remained where I'd left them, jumbled on the floor. I reached down, pulled the leg of my jeans from the pile, fumbled in the hip pocket, deep. It was there. Where I'd put it earlier. I could feel it between my finger and thumb. The captured moments. The captured memories. And I could feel it, the crook of her neck, the angle of her collar bone, the pull of skin over her ribs, her hard concave belly, the way she lay with her arms by her sides and her hands clasped, and her face twisted away from the camera. I slid it out of my pocket. Just a little square of blue plastic and wire and workings. Little bigger than a stamp. Teeny, tiny cogs and wheels of technology. I turned it over into the palm of my hand and closed my fingers round it, closed my eyes, felt the pain of tears, like a boxer.

They kept Maddie in hospital overnight, for observation, they said. Harry left them to it. His heart was shattered, that's what he'll have us believe. A day of organising the dragging of the car out of the canal – British Waterways demanded it – answering some informal questions from the police and some formal ones from school ('Someone tweeted,' said the Principal, was it anything the school needed to be concerned about?). The police gave Harry Maddie's handbag, some wet files and folders that they'd retrieved from the car. Maddie's bits and pieces. And Harry will have you believe that it was all Maddie's fault. Maddie, who's made of trouble and hope and tangled promises. Maddie, who lets the flames lick along the underside, but when you touch the top – and you do – it's still cold. She's still cold. That's Maddie. Anyone can observe that. But the following morning, as he kept to the speed limit on the ring road and the dual carriageway, and the back road towards the hospital to collect her, Harry didn't feel a flicker of guilt any more. In fact, if anything, he felt happy. He says he put the radio on, re-tuned it from the *Today* programme to a music channel playing hip-hop or garage or something, turned up the volume, tapped the steering wheel and nodded his head in time. By the time he pulled up at the lights outside the hospital's main entrance, he looked and felt elated. He'll tell you if you ask. The car was vibrating, it was warm inside and smelt good. He felt in control. And as he braked, a bottle of water, half empty, rolled out from under the passenger seat. Harry says he saw it, watched the intermittent flicker and bow of surface tension on the water as he waited, listened to the tick of the plastic as it rolled gently into view. And, of course, he had to remember – remember the night before. He'd made it into a memory, after all. When the lights changed, he pulled into the hospital car park, into a parking space and switched off the engine. The bottle of water rolled back under the seat, and Harry would have adjusted his mirror so he could see himself. He says he tilted his face, jutted his jaw, licked a finger and flicked away some dried blood from his chin, something sticky from the corner of his mouth. He wanted to remember the night before. He did. The way he tells it, it was simple. A simple transaction. He tells it all now. He says when he'd left the hospital the night before, left hospital staff to it, left them to observe Maddie, he didn't go home.

Not straight away.

The night before, the sky, he'll tell you, had been the colour of steel, and the city was beginning to light up with sprinkles of orange light in the distance. Harry remembers looking at it from his car, biting the skin from round his thumbnail, spitting tiny bits out into the foot-well. He could make out the BT Tower, the Rotunda, like an arty photo – or so he says. There's no point in asking him to explain what he did next. This is Harry Logue we're talking about. The fact is, the hospital car park's CCTV footage will certainly show him driving off in the direction of the city. Harry says he stopped at a petrol station to buy a bottle of water and some baby wipes. He says he put them on the passenger seat and drove into the city and beyond, out past the office blocks and the shopping centres and the promenades of high-rise blocks. He says he didn't need the satnav. And it was dark by that time, a wet, city dark. For a moment, Harry says, he thought he'd be out of luck, thought his chances might be slim, instantly felt his faith crumbling a little. But then he says he saw her, just a blunt outline at first, a little imprecise, emerging like a ghost out of the gloom. All alone, she was. Or seemed to be. Ducking and dipping. And he felt he deserved her. So when he stopped, rolled down the window, felt the smoky night air flush in, she was quite quick. Her skirt, the tightness of it, made it more difficult for her to get into his car and Harry says he noticed her stockings were laddered, but she had a pretty little face, in that light anyway. That's what Harry says. So he shoved the bottle of water and the baby wipes into the foot-well, made room for her, watched her laddered stockings strain against her bony knees as she settled into his car. He's right when he says there are some disused factories round the back of the flats there. Line Works, or Lion Works. Something like that. Kids have set fires against the walls, spray-painted nonsense on corrugated sheets. That's where she directed him. And Harry watched her struggle out of her damp mac, lit, as she was by a weak street lamp, some way off, and he says he watched her hitch up her tiny, tight skirt so she could get at him.

'What's your name?' he remembers asking, but we can guess that with one hand he would have been feeling for the zip of his trousers.

Her face was in silhouette against the night and he says he didn't hear what she said, just felt her dampened hair – a loose pony-tail – between his fingers, then the nape of her neck, her plastic earrings cold on his skin, then her breath on his thighs. Tiny, hot breaths.

'What's your name?' He would have been whispering it, watching the plastic bobble in her hair glinting, and, with his free hand, let's imagine him flicking a couple of little bits of skin off the crumpled material of his trousers, and then twisting and twisting her hair like a rope.

Then, for Harry, it's blurry, incomplete.

The engine was probably still running, and the heater, most likely, cooked the smell of her: cigarettes or something burnt, something spicy. Wet plastic. But the windows would have very quickly greyed out, so all we'd have been able to see was Harry, or the outline of him, head lolled back against the headrest like a drunkard, or like a shadow hardly moving.

He says he doesn't remember the details, though he knew he needed to make this into a memory. He admits he does remember saying, at some point, hearing himself say something like 'Faith. You're a good girl,' or 'Faith. You're good,' or 'very good.' Something like that.

When it was over, he says he drove her back to the corner of the street. Let her have a swig of water from the bottle. She wasn't clean, but she hadn't been messy. He remembers thanking her, giving her an extra fiver, using a baby wipe on his fingers and face when she'd gone. He'll tell us he didn't look back at her as he drove off.

Funny how he remembers feeling himself smile on the way back home. Says he felt like he'd deserved it.

So did Maddie.

That's what he says he remembers.

And that night, he says he slept solidly. No dreams. Duvet undisturbed. His alarm woke him early, and he surfaced into consciousness immediately, blinking in the blue-blackness of the morning, calculating how much of the previous day he could recall, planning out the day ahead. He says he was aware of a smell. Burnt paper, maybe, or the cold. Says he thought he might have left a window open. He checked his watch. Early. Checked his phone. No messages. He lay back down. When he closed his eyes, he'll admit to five minutes of thought about ropes and lions, but he didn't want to take too long. And later, in the bathroom, a wet shave with a new razor for a treat. It should have been a treat, but maybe he was rushing, and he saw the blood form into a bulge, and run off the end of his face into the washbasin before he felt the sharp pang of pain.

That could have spoilt his morning. It could have. He says he tore off a corner of toilet roll, licked it and stuck it on the cut. When he looked at his face in the mirror, it might have been one of his teacher's expressions that looked back at him: all knitted brow and disappointment. That wasn't particularly how he'd have felt. Not then. So he probably spent a moment or two adjusting his expression, lightening his brow, squinting and unsquinting his eyes. He says he noticed he was starting to look old. And ridiculous with that bloody bit of tissue stuck to his chin. Then he looked at his watch, checked the time. Time enough for breakfast. He says he felt hungry. Painfully so. He says he wanted to make the pain into pleasure. He was good at that.

He says he found some eggs – three in a box in the fridge, and two slices of bread, a little stale, in a cupboard. And as he started the process of heating oil in a frying pan and pushing the bread into the toaster, he says he had to keep swallowing in anticipation. When he tapped and cracked each egg, and each egg broke and settled and flapped and hissed into the oil, he says he suddenly realised he couldn't remember the last time he'd eaten. And this fact, this realisation sowed some seeds of anger. Just for a second. Only a second, because he started thinking. This, he was thinking, was how it should be: cooking eggs in his own kitchen because he felt like it. And he prodded the broken yolks of each egg with a spatula, and watched as they spat and spluttered and breathed tiny, nasty, hot breaths at him. If he hadn't noticed the haze of claggy smoke beginning to drift in layers, he says he'd probably have stood there, jabbing at those eggs for a good while longer. Instead, he retrieved his blackened toast from the toaster with a fork, juggled the slices from hand to hand and dropped them onto the work surface, watching, probably a little crestfallen, as they smouldered. But he was hungry, and, with no more bread, charcoaled crusts were his only option. He sighed. Maddie, he remembered, bought that toaster. That was when he says he yanked the toaster's plug from the socket and threw the whole thing upwards and away so it hit the wall cupboard, bounced off and landed sideways on the floor, spilling out powder and crumbs in various livid brown-black messes. Harry admits he kicked it – the toaster, Maddie's toaster – and felt the plastic and metal give, then he scooped the eggs up out of the pan and oozed them onto the toast. He looked at his breakfast. The eggs, still wettish on top, a bit mucousy, not quite cooked, had settled on the toast and were dribbling pale yellow strings down onto the work surface. He hadn't bothered with a plate and it looked like a mess. If he hadn't been so hungry, he'd have left it. But that morning, he was going to eat it. And he did, with his fingers, standing up, letting the stretches of moistness settle like the trails of ghosts across his face.

When he'd finished, he wiped his hands on a tea towel, sidestepped the toaster, and the knife – it was still there on the kitchen floor – but before he left the chaos behind, he says he hesitated at the door. Would Maddie want her handbag? He'd left it on the kitchen table with those still-soggy files and folders the police had given to him.

Not now.

That's what he thought as he slammed the door behind him.

He thought, *Too bad, Maddie.*

And anyway, he says he didn't want his car smelling of canal water.

In Maddie's dreams, she says she was running along the canal towpath. She was running, but she wasn't moving, and her chest hurt from breathing and her eyes felt gritty and she says she could smell something. In her dream, she could smell something like cigarettes or burning meat, or something. And the smell started misting up her thoughts, buzzing through into her brain. When she came to herself, she says it was a moment or two before she noticed the blood, red, on white hospital sheets. And she'd have sat up then, bolt upright, feeling the blood skimming her top lip, her chin, running fast, cooling her skin. She'd have grabbed a handful of tissues from the bedside, and shoved them under her nose, then grabbed some more.

There was a clock on the wall, and she says she could hear it ticking, and in the corridor outside her room, silhouetted figures criss-crossed. Maddie breathed back the blood, closed her eyes.

She didn't call for a nurse. She says she didn't.

Two hours later, maybe more, Harry arrived. She says she saw him from above, through the window, parking the car. Even through the haze of grey morning weather, she says she saw him hesitate, seem to fiddle with something under the passenger seat, then walk, quite fast, through the car park towards the hospital entrance. To Maddie, from that distance, he looked different: older or thinner or something. She says she suddenly wished she was dressed, wished she wasn't wearing a hospital gown, was suddenly aware of the thinness of it, and instinctively gathered the material up at the neck, says she looked around for a dressing gown or a blanket, ended up getting back into bed and pulling the covers up to her chin. And Harry, she says, came into her room in a rush, without knocking. And he stood, just inside for a second, looking at her – looking right at her – and she says she tugged a little harder on the hospital sheets and material of her gown and felt her fingernails digging into the palms of her hands.

'What's the matter with your face?' Harry said after a second or two. 'Your face, there.' And he pointed at her loosely but didn't move any closer.

Maddie says she touched her lip and her cheek, felt the rough dryness of something, and remembered.

'Oh,' and she was shaking her head like she was trying to find the words, 'it was just . . .' Shaking her head like it didn't matter.

She says Harry stood, looking at her, watching her search for an explanation.

'It was . . . nothing,' she said, and she was getting out of bed, her feet, bare and small on the floor, and she says her legs felt heavy, as if she really had been running.

'No.' She remembers Harry stepping towards her, looking closely at her face. 'What is it?'

And his eyes, she says, looked a different colour. Ash grey. And she noticed, she says, for the first time, all those deepening lines at the corner of those eyes. She says she'd never noticed them before. This was the first time, she says.

'Nothing,' she said, and she was looking straight at him, and pushing her hair off her face so that atoms of dust – ever so small, ever so slight – sent silent shadows between them.

Harry would have persisted. He would have pressed her further. He would have, if that nurse, or whatever, hadn't come in just then.

'Ah, Maddie, good, you're awake,' she said, and Harry admits to feeling a spike of disappointment at her smile. 'And you're going home today.'

Then she stopped in her tracks.

'Have you had a nosebleed?' she said.

That would have been when Harry would have noticed the spots of blood on the sheets, and the scrunched-up, bloodied tissues on the bedside table.

'Yes,' Maddie said, and she brushed the answer away with her hand. 'It's OK, I'm fine, really.'

'You sure you're alright?' the nurse asked.

'Yes,' Maddie said, and she wanted to sound brightish. 'Yes, of course.'

'OK, well.' The nurse looked at her watch. 'Doctor'll be here in a while to discharge you. I'm sure hubby here'll help you get dressed.'

'No.' Maddie's voice was sharp, she knew it. She says she tried to force a kind of smile and grabbed some more tissues. 'No. I mean, we're not . . . he's not . . .'

All three of them must have let the sentence die.

'Right.' The nurse looked from Maddie to Harry and back again. Maddie says Harry was biting the skin on the inside of his lip, and the loose tick of the clock filled the silence.

'Well then,' the nurse said, smiling again, 'I'll let you get yourself ready, then.'

When the door closed, Maddie says Harry didn't move.

Maddie says she started wiping at her face with tissues. She says she couldn't look at him – she couldn't look at Harry – but she remembers what he said and how he said it. And his voice, she says it came at her slowly.

'You know, even when you're telling the truth,' he said, 'even when I know for sure you're telling the truth, it feels like you're lying.'

And then, she says he sighed, really heavily, and sat down on the very edge of her bed, focused his words right at her.

'I hate that about you,' he said.

There are posters, word-processed posters, pushed into clear folders and stuck with Sellotape to trees and lamp-posts. Stuck with drawing pins and string to the twisted willow by the canal. *Have you seen?* and *Please contact* and *Everyone misses.* The sentences are crumpled and the ink has bled, spoilt by weather and time. And the picture's blurry.

The picture's always blurry.

It's a fact that we all make wrong decisions. We do. That isn't the problem. In the final analysis, it's what we do to put them right. That's the issue: what we do to put them right.

And we have to put them right. Finally.

The roads weren't good on the way back home. Stop. Start. Roadworks. Underground pipes, or something. The bottle of water clunked, every now and then, against the heels of Maddie's shoes from under the seat. Maddie says it, the journey, all felt a bit like being in a black and white film. There didn't seem to be any colour anywhere. No life. She says she thought it might have been the effects of the Diazepam or sleeping pills or whatever it was they'd given her in the hospital. She remembers wondering if she'd imagined it all. Wondering if she'd imagined, for example, Harry's broken car window – remembers trying to work out when he could have got it fixed. She remembers feeling the burr of queasiness at the thought of the canal, the way the windows of her car shattered and the way her car filled with water, and the way the water smelt of chemicals and tasted of blood, and the way its sticky threads seemed to wind round her, and the way she was desperate to fight back all her instincts. All of them. And breathe. And the way she'd expected blackness, but instead, it was greyish, like breath in winter. And then those men from the factories, the feel of the thick skin of their hands and their strained voices, out of time, pulling and pulling at her, pulling her out of the car, out of the water. And hearing them say it was OK and being pressed against their wet overalls and hearing the tick of their heartbeats and letting them wrap her in a rug or a blanket – something rough – and letting them sit her on a wonky wooden chair in a lean-to factory canal-side office with brown damp patches twisting in the corners of the ceiling, and taking tea from them in a chipped mug and holding it steady in her hands and listening to them telling her how OK it was going to be. Then hearing them talking on the phone and watching the coils of two orange bars of an electric fire fizzing hot and buzzing and feeling a nasty relief at the pain in her chest and her legs and her skin, and asking them about her car. Her car. How was it? How damaged was it? Did they think it would just sink, disappear? And them saying not to worry, it was only a car. Cars are ten-a-penny. It's life that's more important. And then the ambulance people with oxygen and faces with experience of it all. Seen it all before. Nothing new. And calling her their Lovely and their Sweetheart. And thanking the men. Someone thanking the men. And getting into an ambulance, and watching them – the men – light their thin, own-rolled cigarettes. Seeing them heave out breaths in smoke as the doors closed.

She says Harry hadn't spoken, and without her even realising, he'd stopped for petrol. He'd slammed the door so hard, she says she'd been torn out of her memory. Maddie says, as she watched him filling up the car, her mouth felt dry. Hangover-dry. She says she thought she could taste chemicals and wished she couldn't. She felt in her bag, felt her purse, the little bottle of pills from the hospital – painkillers or something – but nothing to drink. So she says she felt under the seat for the bottle, the one that had been rolling out, and felt relieved it wasn't even half empty. And she says the water felt painful to drink, like little razors as she swallowed. But she swallowed. And her lips felt sticky-dry afterwards. And while she rubbed the stickiness away with the back of her hand, she says she half-wondered why Harry was taking so long to pay, and closed her eyes.

She says a gust of cold air took her by surprise, and without speaking Harry slid into the car, flicked a newspaper onto her lap and twisted the key in the ignition. It seemed like a smooth movement, but she noticed the skin under Harry's eye was flickering. Maddie says she noticed it, even through her tacky, tired eyes. She says she unfurled the newspaper, and that's when she saw the picture, professionally taken – clearly – but it was the eyes, grey and not quite looking at her. Then it was the comfortable smile, not quite smiling at her. Then the folded arms and long fingers – a pianist's fingers, maybe – and slim wrists. Then, just visible beneath the cuff of the shirt, the watch: a Patek Phillipe original, if she'd only known enough about watches to recognise a good one. She recognised him, though. Straight away.

She remembers she held the newspaper as still as she could as Harry, with his flickering eyes, stop-started along the B-roads. And she would have read each word of that front-page article with a kind of incomplete numbness we can only imagine in someone like Maddie.

To their neighbours, had they been watching through the net curtains, Maddie's limp might not have looked too serious as she walked down the path towards her front door, and anyway, they might have heard, on the grapevine, some version of her accident. They might have thought they'd got under the skin of it already, though they'd probably have wondered how she could have lost control of her car, even on the ice. Driving so close to the canal? Who does that? It's a towpath, for God's sake, not a road. To their neighbours, as they boiled their kettles, popped their tea bags into their mugs, settled down to watch some telly, most likely, they were thinking the *Express & Star* would report on it one night, and then they'd know for sure.

People are funny. Always half-looking for something to judge.

~

Their house was cold, and, to Maddie, it smelt of wet flannels and cooked food and dust. For the first time, she noticed the front door didn't fit properly, and she had to lean against it hard to close it. She could hear Harry turning on taps, could hear water. She says she wondered if they were going to talk, but couldn't think of a way. She says she wandered towards the kitchen, stood watching him wiping a sponge across the work surface, noticed the toaster upturned in the middle of the floor, the knife, her handbag and some folders on the table. It all seemed to be happening like she wasn't there.

'Have you read this?' she said, eventually, and held out the newspaper.

She says Harry didn't seem to have heard her. His back to her, he seemed to be squeezing out the sponge with one hand into the sink.

'Have you read this article?' she said, and, even to her, her voice sounded dismantled somehow.

'Yes,' he said, but he didn't look at her, 'of course I've fucking read it.'

She would have paused, being able to see his hand from that distance, squeezing and tensing the sponge, seeing the brown water escaping through the cracks between his fingers.

'Well, look. We should talk. We ought to talk about . . .'

'Have I read it?' Harry's top lip was twitching as he turned to her. 'Christ, I'm the one trying to do everything right. Me. I'm the one.'

And he admits he threw the sponge so that it bounced across the work surface and landed where he'd eaten his breakfast.

'Well, you're not doing this right.' Maddie said it in a whisper, but it wouldn't have mattered if she'd shouted it.

'. . . and I'm the one who . . .' Harry remembers clearly he was beginning to snarl and prowl and was running his hand through his hair, all wet now, and he was breathing hard.

'What?' Maddie shouted it; she probably didn't mean to.

And she remembers he looked at her through slitted eyes, all quiet suddenly. His top lip had stretched thin.

'. . . I'm the one who introduced you to everything . . . good.'

Maddie says she let the words settle. Let them settle amongst the crumbs and charcoal.

She would have seemed to think. She'd have furrowed her brow.

'Yeah. Yes.' Harry, he would have approached her slowly. 'Think about it.'

She'd have let her jaw slacken, breathed as if to say something.

'Without me, Maddie' – Harry would have been close to her, she'd have heard the crunch of his feet against the bits on the floor – 'without me, you'd be . . . well, what?'

She says she felt her shoulders tense.

'See.' Harry's fingers, she says she felt them pushing strands of hair from her face. His voice, she says, was softer. 'You need me.'

She says she could smell the damp on his hands.

'I feel sick,' she said.

'You do. You need me.'

'You're making me feel sick.'

'We can get past this.'

'I'm not . . .'

'We can. We can get over it, and get on with our lives.'

'Oh God. I'm going to be sick.'

'You're not. Come here.'

'I'm not doing this any more. I'm not.'

'Sssh. It's OK. It's OK, Maddie.'

'They'll know it was us. The article says he was a student of Gerald's. They'll trace it all back. And what about his watch?

Oh god. We've got it here. I've got it here, in this house. Here. Oh god.'

'Sssh.' He was stroking her hair then, kissing her head – actually kissing it. She remembers it. 'We didn't kill him, did we?'

'That's how they'll get us.' She says her body was still and stiff and her mind was winding up. She says she could feel it winding up. 'That's how they'll link him to us. I tried to get rid of the car. I did.'

'You're not listening.' She says Harry took her face in his hands, directed her gaze slowly, gently, and she says the look in his eyes, it was as if he was from a different existence. 'We didn't kill him.' He said it so quietly, she says she only just heard it.

'We hit him, though. I hit him. With the car . . .' And even saying it, she could probably feel the cogs turning, feel them winding up, maybe.

'Yes,' he said, and it was like he was talking to a child, 'you did. But you didn't kill him. *You* didn't kill him. Did you?'

Then he seemed to let her go. She says he seemed to release her. 'Read the article again,' he said, 'read it now.'

'I can't.' She felt like she was crumpling, like her legs had given up. She says that's what it felt like. 'It's too horrible.'

And then, somehow, she was sitting down, so she says.

'Read it again,' Harry said. 'Out loud. To me.'

She says she didn't. She didn't read it out loud to him. She remembers that. Instead, she scanned it, picked out the highlights again, the bits about the 'vicious attack', 'thought to be the body of Jonathan Cotard,' 'twenty-four stab wounds,' and 'failed attempt to burn the body'.

'It wasn't us,' one of them said, she can't remember which. But she does remember Harry's breath on her ear, on her neck, the tang of his breath, acidic. And the murk in the air might have seemed to lift then. Maybe one of them smiled, in relief or whatever. Perhaps she felt the hard skin of Harry's fingertips skimming the crook of her jaw, and he might have thought he saw a flicker of something familiarish in her eyes, some colour flush into her cheeks. He might have whispered something like, 'Why are you like that? Hmmm?' or 'This is the Maddie I want. This is my Maddie.' Maybe she would have turned her head, kissed the damp palm of his hand, kept her eyes on his, let the pinch of her forehead relax some. And it could have been as Harry leaned across, tilted his head, let his gaze drop to her mouth, pressed his lips against hers – parted, always – that his urgency or disbelief knocked her handbag and those folders and bits and pieces off the table and onto the floor. And Maddie would have dropped the newspaper.

Neither probably cared much. Not then, anyway. They were, most likely, in the moment.

But those moments don't last.

They tick away, just fragments of time.

They mean nothing.

I have to start being honest here, to myself as much as to anyone else.

I got angry. I did. I reacted – still do. But I'm a firm believer in 'first thought, best thought' and I had to do what I had to do. End of. It's just that now and then, the mechanics of it, the whole situation, it gets me down. It's all on my shoulders, I know. It's all down to me to put it back together, get the timing right.

My point being: it has to work. I have to make it work.

Some time back, she came to me, Maddie did, all 'I'm back, I couldn't keep away from you.' All eyes and teeth. She didn't smell right. Her hair, it didn't smell like Maddie. I told her. I said, 'I don't like that scent. Don't wear that scent again.' And she was all 'Don't be like that' and 'I've got something you might like.'

And we both laughed then, and she sat down and crossed and uncrossed her legs and I could see the skin of her thighs.

'Aren't you cold?' I said.

'No,' she said, but there were goose pimples. I could see them.

'No, like I said, I've got something for you.'

She bent down then, unzipped her bag, reached in. From where I was, it looked like she might have been smiling.

'Here,' she said, and she was turning something over in her hand, looking at it. Looking at it the way she looked at me sometimes. Then she handed it to me, held between her thumb and forefinger. Just passed it to me, like it was a prize, like I wasn't expecting it.

'It's for you,' she said, and twitched a nod, all bright.

Even in that light, I could see it was broken a bit. Some of the strap was missing or twisted. She would have known I'd seen that.

'It's working,' she said, as if she was trying to read my mind. 'Listen to it.'

I nodded. I could really smell her, she was so close. Something sharp. Juniper, maybe, or burnt bracken.

'It's working. Listen to it tick,' she was saying, and the tips of her fingers could have burnt my cheeks.

'I'll fix it,' I said.

'I know you will,' she said. 'It's yours now. Keep it.'

And I looked at it like I was pleased, as if I was surprised. And pleased. Like I hadn't expected it. And she held herself unusually still, with just the very edges of a nasty relief in her eyes.

I kissed her then.

I didn't want to, but I did.

≈

Harry's route to work: always the same. No detours. That morning, the next day, he says hail pelted the windscreen and slowed the traffic. That morning the B roads crackled. John Humphrys was probably arguing with some politician, traffic lights probably stayed on red a bit too long, as usual. The same shops, same houses, and the early-bird eager kids walking to school or to the bus-stop.

Yes, Harry slowed – the traffic slowed – next to the bus-stop. He says already two girls waited there, school-girls sheltering from the ice and wet, indistinct behind the blur of perspex. And Harry remembered. He says he couldn't help it. We can imagine how he bit the skin on the inside of his lip and he says he remembered every detail of that time: the girl at the bus-stop with her loose ponytail and big ideas. Yes, he says he pulled on the handbrake, stuck in a queue of traffic, and switched John Humphrys off, flicked through until he found that 10cc track that made her laugh. And as the music filled the car, Harry would have just started to feel a hazy suffocation, maybe, a memory or curiosity. Maybe he might have felt his thoughts uncluttering for a second before the traffic started moving again. And he moved on. He moved on and maybe his thoughts lingered on the notion that he had lost something to that girl. And in that room, in those four white walls that afternoon, in that hotel, on those crisp white sheets, he had needed to take it back. He had. It was a need. Not a want. And it had faded, like the hearts she'd scribed onto the wet perspex of the shelter, like the smell of thick, childish sweat, like the memory of her tears. As he changed into second gear, maybe third gear and as the traffic eased, he might have vaguely wondered if she'd managed to get over it, stop crying, wondered if she'd started concentrating on her GCSEs, wondered if she waited at that bus stop any more.

And the hail had turned into sharp rain by the time he pulled into the school grounds. Slush had blunted the corners of the car park, and as he parked his car, he admits he was thinking about school girls – his 'female pupils' is what he'd say – thinking how miscalculated their thinking was. Walking across the car park, he says he caught sight of Alicia – Aleesha – arriving. He would have smiled to himself. She wouldn't have seen him. But he says he'd barely touched his first coffee in the staff room when the Principal appeared, needing a word. And as he followed, several steps behind, Harry would have been thinking about Maddie, her skin, the memory of it. All that. And the thought of her would have misted up his mind and he would have drawn hearts in the mist of her. So by the time he arrived in that cramped, windowless Principal's office, his impulses would have been dulled, and he wouldn't have been prepared. Thinking about Maddie would have unprepared him.

'There's been a complaint,' the Principal said, not sitting. 'Quite serious.'

Harry says he looked at the Principal and everything seemed to tilt. He says he sat down.

Before Harry had left for work that day, he'd called her 'darling'. And after he'd gone she says it made her laugh. The thought of it made her laugh. He'd never called her that before, and yet she says she realised it was exactly the kind of thing she'd always expected him to say. Lying there in bed, listening to the pellets of hail pelt against the window, she says she laughed. 'See you later, darling,' he'd said, and she'd heard the front door bang closed, then his car start first time, and she'd listened to the crackle of his tyres against icy tarmac and his engine change tone. That morning, he'd worn aftershave; she says she could smell it. She hadn't smelt it in a while. Violets, or ammonia. Something like that. Whatever it was, it made her want to tidy up. She says it made her want to get up and strip the dirty sheets off the bed, tidy up the house, the situation.

Maybe her head was starting to clear as, later, she snapped a black plastic bag off a roll, scooped up the dirty sponge, the junk mail, and, with the edge of her hand scraped bits of dried food off the surfaces. Then – and this is how it must have been – she must have stooped down to pick up the toaster, the knife, the newspaper off the floor; the newspaper, which lay next to her upturned handbag and bits and pieces. She might have been distracted by the headline or the picture, or the *police are still searching for clues*, and maybe this made her throw it – the newspaper – away with the rest of the rubbish.

And for a split second, she would have thought that was it – she had disappeared the problem. She's like that, Maddie is.

She'd have been thinking that Harry was right, they hadn't killed anybody.

Not them.

It was terrible.

What a horrible way to die.

Who would do a thing like that?

No-one deserved that.

Twenty-four stab wounds and then trying to burn the body.

Unthinkable.

And maybe it was then that she saw the folder. It had fallen on the floor the day before, the folder had. A simple, buff-coloured folder, and there it was, on Maddie's kitchen floor. She wasn't quick to pick it up, but, of course, she did.

Her first thought? She says it was whether Harry had looked. Whether he'd looked at these photographs. The photographs in the folder. She tipped them out onto the table. In amongst them, the black and white pull of skin, a face twisted away, hands clasped like a boxer.

And Maddie says she reached into the black rubbish bag

without even thinking, felt around in the rubbish and pulled out the newspaper. She says she wiped off the food and crumbs with the tips of her fingers, and smeared the wetness across the paper. And she says wet lines rose like swollen scratches across the words, across Jonathan's face, worn grey by then and almost indistinct. She says she stood for a while, trying to make out his features, trying to remember something he'd said, the timbre of his voice. But she says she just couldn't. She could only remember the last time she'd thought about it. And she says she felt confused. Confused, or sick.

To think, if the doorbell hadn't rung, she might have remembered. Or she might have flicked through the newspaper and read page 8.

She says at first, she wasn't going to answer it, the door. She was going to ignore it. But the doorbell rang again, and then again. And each time, she felt her stomach tighten a bit more.

When she answered, she had to pull at the door hard. The damp, or something, had warped it. And she says it was a man, youngish, at the door, outside her door, wearing a uniform.

'Ms Harper?' he said, and the thought must have flitted into her mind that she might deny it. Deny being her. Deny all of it. But before she could think, or speak, he must have held out a wallet, an identification card. Police. And she says he seemed to be telling her who he was and smiling and flicking hailstones off his shoulder and asking to come in.

Maddie says she wondered what he'd think of her, what he'd think of the house, the mess. And she hadn't taken a shower.

'Nice house,' he said as she let him in, but Maddie says he had to shift some of Harry's paperwork – marking or something – and some tissues and bits and pieces of change before he could sit down on the sofa in the living room.

She says she sat opposite him and the noise of the hail stones on glass and on concrete outside – the temporary violence of the sound of it – calmed her, and she realised she was still holding the newspaper.

'Right. So.' He felt for something in his pocket: a notepad. 'How are you then?' he said.

Maddie. How are you?

And dust motes, imagine how they floated in the air in silent fury.

'OK,' he said before she answered, and she was certain she saw him glance at the newspaper in her hand. 'Do you want to tell me what happened,' he said, but to Maddie, it didn't sound like a question.

Maddie says she felt like she might have looked a bit drunk, and she says he leaned forward, lowered his voice.

'Take your time,' he said. 'Start at the beginning.'

At the beginning. Where's the beginning?

So this was it then. This is what Maddie was thinking. This raker-over of coals, this young turner-over of stones sitting opposite her with eyes settled on her, was it.

'Was it icy?' he said, very quiet.

She says she nodded and half thought – actually admits to half thinking – about making some kind of pass at him. Christ Almighty, she says she hated all this. And she says she had to tear her thoughts apart. Get them out. She says she had to search across the ceiling and into the top corners of the room to find the sequence of events.

'We'd had a row,' she said, 'an argument. I said some nasty things.'

I am, she would have been thinking, so bored, and I'm so glad you're here. You asked me *was it icy?* It's always icy. I'll tell you how it happened, she must have been thinking.

'I was driving fast, too fast. Then I felt a bump and wasn't sure. It was dark. I couldn't have stopped. I don't think I could have stopped.'

Just saying the words was killing the pain. She says she hadn't realised how much she wanted to hear herself say them, had almost forgotten how painfully bored of it she thought she was.

And she must have been like a molecule just on the edge of reacting. Just on the very, very edge. And Jonathan's face, it was there, almost smiling up at her from the newspaper. The whole time. It was her fault, she realised, all her fault. And she says she took a breath in and looked at him, this policeman, with his damp shoulders, and she says she just wanted him to do it. Just do it. Just say it. She wanted to confess and make him arrest her. She did. And she says her eyes felt hot.

'I didn't mean to hurt him,' she said.

She says the officer put his notebook or whatever it was he was holding down, she says a flicker of uncertainty crossed his face.

'Your car?' he said. Something like that.

Maddie wasn't really listening to him then, though, and she says she picked up the newspaper, was thinking *I'm responsible for this man's death. I ran him over and drove off. Surely I'm responsible.* She probably felt the words bubbling up, felt her throat tightening, her lips moving. And then – and this is how she describes it – she heard a bang, and the sound of heels striking the tiled floor of the hall, and he came, as if summoned by a guardian angel – just materialised in the room. Harry. He swept in, bringing outside-cold with him. That's how Maddie describes it.

'You didn't close the door properly,' Harry said, then, noticing the policeman: 'Oh, Christ.'

'It's alright, sir,' the officer stood up. 'Just taking a quick statement from Ms Harper, about the accident.'

Maddie says she knew Harry was trying not to look at her. She says his hair was wet and his eyes were wide and she could see the black inside lining of his mouth.

The officer said something like, 'Just routine. We won't be taking it any further.'

Maddie says she felt the room jolt.

'British Waterways will want you to remove the vehicle from the canal, though.' the officer said, moving to the door. 'Written off, I expect.'

'I expect.' Harry would have looked like he'd been slapped. Imagine it.

'Oh, well. It's only a car,' the officer said. Then he looked at Maddie and, before he left, said, 'You take care. No need to get upset about a car.'

Maddie says she felt horribly cold as she heard the front door slam shut.

Night time isn't easy. It's hard being in control. Too many thoughts. Too many ifs and buts. Too many connections to make. And this. Doing this, living like this – having to live like this – is like plunging into cold water, every time. Sometimes I can't think clearly – and I know I'm being sketchy – sometimes I don't know how, or if, to simplify it. I like the happy coincidences that just crop up. Take the watch, for instance. Maddie reached out, reached through, handed it away from herself. It's in my hand now, I'm turning it over, looking at the inscription that she probably didn't notice: 'From Gerald, be proud.'

And then there's Faith, isn't there? Always there, in the darkness somewhere, tethered safely in the past. She, who wanted to be a doctor, travel the world.

I should feed her really.

Let's just say there's a picture of her in the newspaper

somewhere. Page 8. My slip-up. But a useless left-hand page that no-one really reads. No-one would really notice the 'say cheese' smile, or the ropes and a lion on the school blazer, anyway.

What Maddie remembers is Harry standing looking out of the window. She says he seemed to be looking out onto the street, watching the policeman leave, looking at the water, the wet concrete and slabs and tarmac. The hail had just started again and the air in the room was prickled with sourness, with toxins, and all of it was in him, in his mouth, in his lungs, in his blood. And there was only a hint of expression, just a hint, around his eyes. Poison around his eyes. He said something like, 'How did it come to this?' Something like that.

Behind him, Maddie, sitting on the edge of an armchair, sealed-off, not moving, not even blinking. Picture it. She says she could hear a vague whirring, buzzing noise, like a sort of tinnitus in her head, like she could hear the workings of her brain, or someone's brain, all grinding away.

'Fucking hell,' Harry said, and it made her jump.

Then she says he was shaking his head, shoving his hand through his hair, saying 'I've been suspended. Fucking suspended from my job.' And he was sitting down hard on the sofa saying 'Unbelievable' again and again. He was holding a letter. A single sheet. Maddie could see it trembling. She says she wanted to ask if she could read it, but Harry had hold of it and his eyes were flicking across the words, his top lip was thin.

'Look at this.' She says he slapped the letter with the back of his free hand. 'Look . . . *you have knowingly misled your Faculty and Senior Management regarding year 11 attainment . . .*' She says his voice was high and loud, and he was shaking his head again, breathing as if he'd been running.

'What does that mean?' Maddie remembers saying. 'I don't understand what that means.'

'Christ.' Harry was standing up again, and the shadow of falling rain or hail might have coloured him grey. 'They think I lied about some kids' fucking GCSE coursework.'

Maddie says it sounded as if his mouth was full of spit and she watched him sit down again, rubbing his temples with his thumb and forefinger.

'Did you?' Maddie's voice seemed ages away to her. And she says he looked at her. Looked straight at her face.

'No,' he said, and she says he sounded calm.

'Then why would they say it?' Was she smiling at him? She says she couldn't tell.

'I don't know.'

'Think.'

The light was dim in that room but Maddie says she could see his mouth opening, his lips, silvery; says she could hear him swallowing. He didn't speak.

'You must know if you've lied.' Even she could hear the smile in her voice then, she says she could.

'Christ, Maddie.'

'Well, did you?' She would have been leaning forward, like she does. She says she was enjoying it. To her, she seemed to be enjoying it, and even in the dark, she wanted him to see it.

'No, no. No, I didn't.' She says she could see the whites of his eyes, the reflection of rain or hail in them. 'I think . . . I don't know . . . it's about their fucking folders. Folders full of shit work . . . I might have lost . . . misplaced one, or two . . . everybody does it, everybody . . . but, suspended . . . suspended from my job . . . I just . . .'

She says it was like he couldn't look at her. She didn't move.

'But I swear to you, Maddie, I didn't lie. I didn't.'

Maddie says it was like the distance between them was too

much for him, and as he started massaging the bones of his temples again, she left him, left the room, that is. She says she could just about feel herself smiling, just about hear her own footsteps as she walked upstairs, and into her room, and even though the clock on her bedside table glowed barely midmorning, all she wanted to do was sleep. There were those sleeping pills, or tranquillisers, from the hospital. She had a little bottle of them. She says she shook a couple of pills out, swallowed them without water. She says there was newsprint on her fingertips, on the palm of her hand, and she dropped the newspaper and stepped on it as she peeled off her dress, dropped that on the floor. She says all she wanted to do was sleep. Sleep it away. And she probably doesn't remember falling asleep, the act of falling asleep, but, in her dreams, there was a tow path and a canal. She was running. Running again. And she couldn't breathe, and she felt trapped – a feeling of being trapped – a twisted feeling of not being able to move away from the pain, a tightness. It was as if she was in the grip of it, the situation, as if it had a hold, a tight embrace over her. And there was a kind of pulsing, and somewhere in that dream there were complicated flickering patterns, reflections of water on a wall, maybe, and dim twitches of desperation and despair and a heavy paralysis of something like guilt, and a desire – an intoxicating tug – no, a real need for it all, all of it, to be over. Finished.

It wasn't finished, though. How could it be? And later, some time later, when Maddie woke up, surfaced slowly into the fractured blackness of her reality, she says she felt hot, clammy, wet with sweat or something. The duvet cover was stuck to the back of her legs. The top of her head ached, and the muscles of her thighs. She says she sat up, pushed the duvet away, felt the room sway and the crush of disappointment at being there, in that house, in that situation. Red numbers on the clock said 5 or 8, she couldn't be sure, her eyes ached. She says she made herself stand and found she was trembling. Through her reflection in the glass of the window, she could see only the bluntest of outlines. Under her feet, Jonathan's face, if only she knew it, and coming from somewhere, the sound of a television. Not her television, a neighbour's. A newsman's intonation. She'll tell us she leaned her head slowly to the side, heard the internal crackles, vaguely wondered if anyone could see her, if anyone was looking from outside at the curve of her hip, the outline of her breasts. She says she gathered her hair up off her neck, bunched it up on top of her head, felt the air cool the skin on her shoulders, felt the little hairs stand up on her arms, her armpits. And she took a deep breath, and felt the thin flesh of her chest stretch, let her hair down and could make out the ripples of her ribs with her fingertips. Somewhere there, very vaguely, she says she ached. She thought it might have been some kind of delayed reaction from the accident – the accidents – or the sleeping pills. She didn't know what exactly.

Her dress was crumpled on the floor, partially covered in a couple of tissues and bits and pieces. She says she slid it over her head, the dress, felt the material catch and stick to the flesh of her back, the arch of her spine. There was a taste in her mouth she says she didn't like, so she went downstairs into the kitchen. She says the house felt empty and the kitchen had a sweetish smell about it, like burnt honey, she says, or liquid smoke. And it was a mess, still, so it took a moment or two for her to notice. Took a moment or two for her eyes to adjust to the electric light-bulb light. Amongst the debris, on the table, there was a whiskey bottle, less than half full, with its top missing. She says she picked up the bottle, sniffed at it. Burnt honey and liquid smoke. She says it made her feel queasy, and she allowed a flutter of agitation to pass, like a wave, through her head at the thought of Harry drowning his sorrows amidst all that mess. Her agitation would have sharpened her momentarily, and she would have noticed the glass over by the sink, an inch of brown liquid in it. She says the feeling was like a breeze of hatred. *God*, she thought, *he can't finish anything*. And she snatched at the glass, poured the whiskey away, says she felt the muscles of her face tighten as she watched it settle and stain. *Whiskey. So, Harry has turned to drink now.* That was what she was thinking. And she says her thoughts were tightening, twisting up. That Harry had been suspended from his job was bad enough, but if he was going to start drinking now, if she was going to have to cope with that on top of everything else, well, she wouldn't. She couldn't cope with that. She'd leave him, again. She knows how to disappear herself, at least for a little while. Everybody does. And it was whilst she was in this frame of mind, at the edge of a decision, a decision coloured by what she had done, what they had done: everything she'd done. Jonathan, Harry's suspension, the brown threat of whiskey pooling in the sink, the lying about folders, missing folders – missing folders – that she saw it.

And she says it was as if she lifted her head and was directed straight to it. There, amongst the mess on the kitchen table: a buff-coloured folder. The folder she had taken from Jonathan's boat, Jonathan's bedroom. And it was on her kitchen table. She says she panicked, wondered for a second if Harry had seen it, seemed to remember it sliding onto the floor. Had she picked it up and put it on the table? She says she couldn't remember, says her head felt fuzzy again, and she loathed herself for that. She looked at it, the folder, says she ran her fingers over the cold smoothness of it, traced the word written in biro on the front: 'Madeleine'.

She says she thought, *it's 'Maddie'. Nobody calls me Madeleine any more. Nobody.*

Harry had sat for hours in that living room after Maddie had

left him – left the room – gone padding upstairs after the police officer had left. It seemed like hours to him, that's what
he says. Hours of rubbing the bones of his temples, hours of
re-reading the letter from the school. Hours of watching the
hail turn to rain and back to hail again. And that Maddie had
walked away from him, that she had questioned him, and that
he had felt he had to swear he hadn't lied. And still, she had
walked away, without glancing back once.

The truth was he hadn't misled school, not about missing
folders or students' grades. He hadn't. And in the silence of
that living room of theirs, he listened to his own breathing, his
own swallowing. He said he thought surely it wasn't just about
folders. He says he thought there must have been something
else, some other reason. He says he thought they must have
found out about Jonathan, or that time with the girl. He'd
known she wasn't sixteen. He says he felt sure they must have
found out. Someone must have told them.

He says his forehead felt greasy against the tips of his
fingers. He says he felt like he needed help, needed comfort,
needed someone, something. He says the darkness in the room
was choking him. Closing in. That's why he says he went into
the kitchen, flicked on the light, found the Christmas whiskey.
He says he was glad it was only half empty, poured an inch
or so into a glass, swigged some of it. He says it felt painful
to drink, like little razors as he swallowed, and he held onto
the sink as he coughed some of it up, felt his tongue and lips
burning and tried to wipe the feeling away with the back of
his hand. He says he closed his eyes and wished he wasn't such
a lightweight, wished he could go back to the start, take a
different route, wished he could make it different, wished for
the Maddie, his Maddie, who laughed as she read him those
dirty stories she'd written. When he opened his eyes he was
still thinking about Maddie, and his thoughts were tinged with

regret, and it hurt him. That's what he says. It hurt him that she had become such hard work, when it had all started off so easily. Even after all these years, it hurt him to have to work so hard with her. Hurt him to have to work so hard to keep her. The effort of it, he says, was exhausting. And it was that exhaustion, he says, that made him say things, sometimes, do things, sometimes, forget things. The exhaustion she created in him. She created it. Yet when she left him that time, disappeared for a year or so, he'd almost collapsed under the weight of grief. He'd never even tried to replace her – not seriously. More than a year without her. He'd never managed to rationalise that. And even there, in that kitchen, the thought of her leaving him – having left him – still ground into his thoughts like poison, as if just the thought of it, the memory of it, was a living organism, an endless contamination. And Harry says he took a long swallow from the whiskey bottle, sucked a quick in-breath through gritted teeth, let the feeling settle, let his breathing steady, put the bottle on the table. And it was then, at that precise moment he says he saw the folder. Right where Maddie had left it, on the table. And tipped out, onto the table, were photographs. Harry says he only noticed them amongst the other bits and pieces after a second or two, and even then, the way the light shone – electric light – the way it reflected the history of misted fingerprints, blurred the images, made them difficult to see, to focus on. And Harry picked the first one up in slow motion, squinted-in the familiarity of the pull of her skin, felt his brain calibrating and recalibrating against the recognition of her face, even though it was a face twisted away as if in pain, or joy, he couldn't tell. And her hands, in tight fists, the way she'd always done, the way he knew she'd always done. He says he held each photograph in mechanical turn, his grip distorting each a little. He says he rubbed the very tip of his thumbs against the muted finger marks that smothered the flat, stretched flesh beneath them. And he says he felt an effort, like a gradual ecstasy of realisation, as if he had managed to turn over a heavy stone in a damp cave and had blocked the only exit. And he was there for a while, so he says, just looking, just allowing himself to realise. To enjoy the pain of it. He says it was like he was seeing things finely. And he says he felt he had no choice. None. At the time. And he slid the photographs into the folder, left it on the table, left the bottle of whiskey and the mess, and as he crept up the stairs, to anyone who could see, he might have looked like a man experimenting with several possibilities in his head.

In fact, looked at from a certain angle, you could probably see the strain in every movement he was making, the strain to miss the creaking step on the stairs, the strain not to rattle the banister or to let the pressure of his weight vibrate the air and resonate into her room. When the bedroom door clicked – the lock, or hinge, or whatever made that clicking sound – he would have winced, inhaled, frozen as if his stillness would undo that sound. And he would have seen her lying in the darkness. Would have just been able to make out the shape of her. Maddie. In bed. And he would have been surprised that she didn't stir. He says it was like she was in a coma. Her breathing, her breaths, were long and every now and then she murmured a sort of quiet note like a piano slightly out of tune. So Harry says. And he felt the need to step closer to her, to listen. Beneath his feet, he knew her dress and the newspaper and her bits and pieces muted any sound. The room was moonless and sunless, only a dim red glow from the clock gave her an outline, but he says the pull of skin on her neck and her face twisted away was clear to him, even in that light. He says he reached out to touch her face, and she seemed to let him. He says he could smell a cat-like, chemical smell and wished he couldn't, and he tried to suppress his breathing, his heartbeat.

He says he felt like he was borrowing her trance. That's the phrase he uses. Borrowing Maddie's trance.

He says he called her name. 'Maddie,' he said, but not loudly.

She didn't even move.

He says he rested his hand, the palm of his hand on her shoulder, and she remained still, though he knew his skin was cold on hers. Without the sound of her breathing, Harry says he might have thought she was dead.

'Maddie,' he said, louder this time, and he could feel the bones of her shoulder under the tightness of her skin. Somewhere nearby there was a voice, so he says, a wiry intonation with words running into words like a smooth, persistent buzz. He says he stood up then, heard paper crumple under his feet, unclipped his belt buckle and zip with one hand, let his trousers fall off him and onto the floor, onto her bits and pieces. Even then, she still didn't move. With each button of his shirt he still thought she might wake, and as he grabbed a handful of tissues from the box on her bedside table, he still thought it. When he slipped into bed, he says he could feel his skin warming in the muffled heat of her, as if he was being smothered by a damp tea-towel, and he says he thought he might have felt her rouse, might have felt an alteration in her breathing. He says he might have. But he sort of knew she was sound asleep. That she was unaware. He guessed she must have taken some pills then. And so he says he let himself skim the tiny hairs on her arm, the skin of her waist, her hip, her thigh. Then, slowly, he says he let the very tips of his fingers – the very tips – skim the ripples of her ribs, and then the intermittent line that was her spine, and, he says, he traced a heart shape on the warm flesh of her back with his finger. And then slowly, so as to be absolutely sure not to wake her then, he let his hand touch her breast. He says it felt small. A small breast, like a girl's not a woman's. And he'd have been pleased about that. He admits to squeezing the thin flesh. Squeezing and pressing his chest against her back, maneuvering himself so that the point of his elbow rested on her hip, then very slowly pushing his knee up to the softened muscles of her thighs. He says he could smell she hadn't washed her hair, let his nose rest on the nape of her neck so she would be able to feel his skin, his breath, blowing, touching. And he says her skin tasted of sherbet and salt, and this was the Maddie he wanted. This was his Maddie. And he says he only meant to hold her, his Maddie, but he held her tightly, found he was more than embracing her, he was gripping her as if it was a necessary tightening of a ligature. He knew it was twisted but he says it was more complicated than that. He says he, they, were victims of pace. If he didn't seize her, seize the moment, well . . . he can't explain. He isn't stupid by any means, but he says he just felt he'd lost something to Maddie, that she had taken something from him – kept on taking something from him, and there, in those four walls, it was a need. That's what Harry says. To him, it was a need. And he seems to need to explain. Explain himself. He says the fact that Maddie didn't object, didn't cry out, means he can't have hurt her. He admits she felt limp, empty. He'll admit that he felt compelled by the smell of her – that salty, sweet, thick smell of her. He remembers looking down at the outline of her legs, seeing the backs of her knees, and he remembers pulsing with remorse soon after, feeling like the kind of man everyone hates. And he says he felt that familiar, sick, claustrophobic dizziness. He remembers leaning his face against her shoulder as he clung to her, feeling her hair greasy-damp with his tears. He'll tell more, but at that moment, he says he knew exactly what he was. And he says he felt the room, the darkness, the clogged air, closing in on him. And he says he felt as if he just needed to get out, get away. Go. He says Maddie's skin looked oddly bluish in the failed light, and as he moved himself off her, as he felt himself unstick from her, as he gathered up his clothes and left the room, he says the sound of her breathing was suffocating.

The worst part? It's waking up every day without her. Waking up and she's not there. Every day. Every one of those five thousand days or so. I can still smell her on the sheets, on the pillow, in the air. I wake up and feel her. Feel the bones of her, her muscles, her flesh. And every day it kills me. It's like living with a ghost. It is. I'm not letting that happen again. Not after what happened with Harry. Especially after that. So, it's a no-brainer. He says he didn't know, but he's bound to say that.

Look, it's just about making them realise. Realise they can't treat people this way. They can't. They can't treat me this way. They can't treat Faith this way. And even though everything's almost ready, I still think about not doing it, I still think I might change my mind. And then last week, she came to me, Maddie did, she came to me when she'd finished work, and she just looked at me.

'You've lost weight,' I said.

'Yes,' she said, 'I forget to eat sometimes.'

I stood up, closed the door, locked it. 'Well,' I said, 'try to remember.'

'I'll try,' she said, and she was next to me, 'I will, I'll try.'

Her hand was on my arm, I could see she'd started biting her fingernails again and I wondered what had started to go on in her head. Her eyes were telling me something, but I wasn't sure what. And her pupils were dilating slowly and there was barely a flicker of her eyelids.

'Why do we live like this?' she said. 'Why do we keep doing it?'

Maddie says there was something about the light in their bedroom that meant she couldn't avoid seeing her reflection, couldn't avoid seeing her own reflection running fingers across the newspaper, across the headline and the picture, across the black and white of it, across that left-hand page, page 8, across the ropes and lion and the smile. The reflected smile. Says she couldn't avoid seeing her reflection everywhere. Says it seemed as though it was in the glass of the bedroom window, in the sheen of wood on the wardrobe door, in the scratched metal of the door handles. Ghosts of herself, all over the room. Ghosts, emptying drawers, taking clothes from hangers, ghosts not even folding those clothes, instead, bundling them into a hold-all. An audience of ghosts, aping her movements, distorting the shape of her. Ghost hands grabbing her bits and pieces, her clothes, essentials, and packing, pushing the clothes into the bag, pushing them and watching the bag bulge with all the bits and pieces.

The folder, the one with the photographs, was on their bed. Every now and then, a ghost would stretch out a hand and almost touch it, so Maddie says. Almost, but not quite. And she says she stopped for a second, took a breath, looked at the bag and the folder and the newspaper, noticed the thin ghosts hesitate, says she felt them judge. From somewhere far off, she probably recalled the pains, the pull of her past, maybe. She might have felt an odd, nostalgic jolt. But we all know that couldn't last, and anyway, it was too late then. She didn't hear Harry – she says she didn't hear him – come back from wherever he'd been. She says she didn't hear him slam the door, or his footsteps on the stairs, didn't see him peering in at her. So, when he spoke, it made her jump.

'What're you doing?'

And he was standing between her and the ghosts. She says he was standing, then he was holding her shoulders, slowly looking at her face, searching hard, eyes flickering.

'What're you doing?'

And she says his grip tightened on the words, on her, and she had to shake and twist to release herself. And, she says, she didn't answer, just shook her head, and pushed at those clothes in the bag.

'You're not leaving me,' Harry said.

And the sound of Maddie zipping the bag probably cut right through them both.

'You're not. You're not leaving me again,' he said.

And we can imagine how he'd have tried to stand in her way, maybe unzip the bag, maybe empty her bits and pieces on the bed. We can guess that awkward dance they would have done again, the desperate, uncoordinated rhythm of it. We can see it all, if we try: Maddie, trying to worm her way out of his grip, and the narrow, grey slashes in the air between them; something brewing in Harry's facial expression, in his eyes – a rapid, faint rhythm of something – a flutter, or a quickening, something in the distance. And both of them saying things, using their voices like a cloak, trying to hide things and reveal things at the same time. Bad magicians. Bad. And it will have been exhaustion that stopped them. Exhaustion that made Harry sit down hard on the bed, breathe fast, do his 'I love you' routine again and again, his words spilling upwards at Maddie, trying to show how much he could reveal as she struggled with the zip of her bag. Both of them grasping, releasing and grasping again.

'You don't have to go,' he was saying. But Maddie says she was sure she did have to go, at that point.

'If it's about these photos. If it's about these pictures. Christ. I mean, Maddie, it doesn't matter.' And he had hold of the folder, and he was looking up at her, and he says her face changed, like she'd been reversing too fast and had put on the brakes. Outside, then, it might have been day or night, and Maddie's ghosts were looking in. And Harry says he sort of seized the moment, stood up, tried to hold her, tried to say it would be OK, that the photographs really didn't matter, that she looked beautiful – she was beautiful – that he loved her, every bit of her, that everyone makes mistakes. Everyone. Even him. He says he drew a long breath to tell her, to explain. He'd got it, all of it, all the words he was ready to reveal, to uncloak. Some to hide, some to reveal. But he was ready, ready to tell her about his mistake.

Maddie says she remembers feeling nausea pull at her, and she swallowed it away, looked at Harry's hand, with its crinkle of thick blue veins, and the folder gripped between his white fingers. She says she let her eyes stray up to his face, watched his lips moving. Could see his lips moving but his voice was blurred. And behind him, the mirror on the wardrobe. She says there was a chip or a little crack at the top she hadn't ever noticed before, and beneath it, the face of a ghost who might have been crying.

And then, Harry's lips stopped moving. Maddie says she saw them stop, says his chin seemed to be quivering, says she noticed he hadn't had a shave. She says she can't remember clearly but might have said something like, 'The photos matter, Harry. They do. They matter.' And Harry's chin probably stopped trembling then.

I told her once she reminded me of a cat, a stray, prowling around stealing other cats' food, sleeping in other cats' beds. I don't know if she was listening.

Time after time she'd told me she didn't know what love was, Maddie, or even if it existed.

But I knew what love was.

I did.

I do.

One day she asked me how I could possibly like her after all that she'd done. I told her I loved her. It was love that I felt. Love, for god's sake. She sat for a while looking down at her toes. I thought we were close then. Close to making it perfect. *Time*, I thought, *give her time*.

When I asked her, and I did a thousand times, she said she would need to go back to Harry. She needed to go back to him.

She said he gave her what she deserved.

But in those days, in those early mornings I'd watch her. Watch her breathing. Watch her growing. Just watch.

I had faith in her then.

And even when I gave her the choice, even when she chose him, I still thought I knew. And I believed she'd come back. Surely.

There were days when she loved me, I swear, days when she liked me more. I could tell. I can always tell.

It was just me and Maddie, even after Faith.

Once she told me if it hadn't been for Faith, she'd probably have stayed with me. I've never told anyone that. Never. Sometimes, thinking about that makes me feel sad. Angry.

I've always hated Harry.

Now, after what he's done, after all he's done to us, it's much more than hate I feel.

So.

It's warm down here. I keep it warm. You can feel the sweat on your back all the time. I keep it warm down here. It's only right. Faith has sometimes seemed happy. We have talked. She is my salvation, really. There is no superiority between us. She had the right to be human, she knew that. I don't insult her.

But she did disobey.

She's a bright girl, just like her mother, if only she knew, just like Maddie Harper. If she had been a decent girl, none of this would ever have happened. We all know that. She said it was only partly her fault though, that mainstream culture made her like it. But look what she was wearing. Look. I leave it all hanging up: the thin material of the blouse is tacky and grimy now, and the skirt, with its creases at the waistband where she hitched it up and folded it on her way to school. It would have been long enough if she'd left it alone, worn it properly.

I trusted her. I did. Like I trusted Maddie. Now, it just feels like I was a fool. Like I've been made a fool of.

And I say to her, I say, 'Faith, is it just in your nature?' And she has told me again and again that nature and nurture aren't alternatives. She has a point. But I'm sure I've seen her, sometimes, looking at that school blazer – the lion and ropes – and even with her limited movements, picking away at something at the hem, or scratching at a stain on the sleeve. And, I swear, there's been no regret in her eyes.

And it's that, that sort of behaviour, that's when I can't help thinking they're too much alike, aren't they? I can't help thinking *stop pretending to be your mother. Don't ever do that.*

At night, it was – is – quiet. And, in truth, I think only of Maddie. I try not to. I do. And it's like she's hit me, beaten me until I'm lying in a pool of my own blood on this floor.

Maybe she's right about love, Maddie is. Maybe it is overrated.

Harry's weak. Weakening.

He says his face was turned away from her, Maddie. Says he couldn't look at her in their bedroom as she was struggling with the zip on her bag. Says the muscles in his neck ached. Says a couple of hot tears dripped onto the back of his hand, onto the folder he was carrying. Says once he started he couldn't stop. His face, he says, was turned away from Maddie, turned away from what she'd said.

'I don't make promises, Harry,' he remembers picking out from it all.

She didn't make promises, Maddie didn't.

And he says he wanted to speak, say something profound, but he could just hear somebody crying, and says he felt himself stuck, as if in a kind of tight alley with razors of guilt embedded in the cracks of the crumbling walls.

'Are you listening?' Maddie said. And Harry says he glanced up at her then and he says her eyes looked shiny black, like plastic, like the eyes of someone who deserves not to be around.

We can't blame him for thinking that.

We can only blame him for what he did. Blame them all.

And Maddie was talking to him. Telling him, at last. Thinking it was all going to be OK for her.

Faith ate like a bird, started pushing the food I gave her around the dish, started losing weight. She sometimes looked at me when she thought I couldn't see, and her eyes looked big in the candle-light. There always was a blackness in the corner of those eyes, specks of grit or something. She had a pad and pen. I gave her those so she could put down in writing, see exactly what she'd done, in words. Or pictures. She needed to take responsibility – we need to take responsibility – she knew that. She hasn't written anything.

But now they have to take responsibility. Most of it. They need to take most of the responsibility.

It's a mess.

It's all a mess.

They tried to get rid of us, like a nasty stain. They tried to scrub at us.

But we're still here.

From a certain angle, a certain viewpoint, look. Look, and we're still here.

Maddie says the kitchen floor felt sticky, cold under her bare feet. She'd gone down there and says she was drinking tap water out of a cup and it tasted hard, like chemicals and she couldn't seem to swallow it quickly enough, so her teeth ached from the cold of it. She says her heart was beating fast and she felt empty from talking and she had to hold on to the round metal edges of the sink to keep herself steady, and she had the newspaper clamped under her arm. Close to her.

Harry had followed her downstairs, Maddie says. When she looked at him, when he came into the kitchen where she was, she says he seemed all eyes and neck. She says he watched her swallow the water, and she says she could predict what he would say.

'You have a child? Maddie? A child? And you left that child to come back to me?'

Maddie says she ran more water into the cup, watched it splash over her hand, licked the corners of her mouth with her tongue. Cold.

And Harry, he was sitting down when she looked, sitting at the kitchen table, and when she looked at him, she said he seemed to be calculating something complicated. When he spoke again, she says he turned to her slowly and she could see one of his eyelids twitching.

'Why are you telling me now?' he said, and his voice sounded flat.

Maddie says she swallowed more water, felt cold drips down her chin, knew droplets were growing on the material of her dress, looked down at the newspaper clasped between her arm and her ribs, but didn't speak.

'And her father,' Harry said. And he shifted round in the chair, clasped his hands together, rested his elbows on his thighs. Maddie says she saw the bald patch on the top of his head and heard him say something like 'Christ' or 'Stop'. She says she put the cup on the side, wiped her mouth on a tea towel, leaned back against the sink.

'Who was it? Who is it? The father. Who is he?' Harry's voice had lost all strength, according to Maddie. We can hear the weakness in every word.

Maddie says she shook her head, told him that wasn't important. Something else was important. Maddie says she didn't think she owed him too much of an explanation. At the time, she didn't feel like explaining much. But maybe we all know how those situations go. And Harry might have been on his feet then, asking about the father, asking 'Why now? Why are you telling me now?' And Maddie says something about how her skin felt bad, peculiar, and says she was aware she was taking only shallow breaths.

'She's missing, Harry. She's gone missing. It's in the newspaper.'

She says Harry snatched the newspaper from her. His lips still moving fast, saying something about how they had to 'sort things out', asking questions about how she could have done this to him, telling her to explain herself. All these years she'd been lying, keeping it from him. All these years he'd thought that time when she'd left him she was travelling, not fucking about, having bastard children, saying what a bitch, what a whore, what a fucking cunt she was. And even as he was saying all this, even as the inside of his mouth flushed with saliva and bits of spit flew out and white bubbles of it fizzed and burst on Maddie's skin and on the newspaper, Maddie says she knew what she had to do. She says she could see Harry's fingers pressing into the headline, into the picture.

The missing school girl, the blazer with ropes and a lion. She says she thought about explaining how, all those years ago – fourteen? No, fifteen – when they left university and he'd driven her mad with his neediness, his obsession with her, his bloody teacher training, and how she'd looked at him that morning all those years ago and that the thought of having to spend the rest of her life with him scared her into leaving there and then. Packing and leaving. Leaving a note. Gone. Yes, she thought about explaining how she had intended to travel the world, maybe never return, maybe re-train as a doctor or something useful. She thought about telling him that. She thought about telling him she'd only managed to get as far as Birmingham. But she knew there were some bits she'd edit out. About how she'd had to survive, how she'd had to earn money for a good while. She would never tell him that. She wouldn't tell him about where she'd had to live, how she'd had to live, the working girls she'd had to work alongside, the long dark nights dipping and diving, cat-and-mousing. She wouldn't tell him about all the men. She might have told him she didn't want the child. She'd never wanted a child, any child, let alone in those circumstances. She'd have told him that. She would. She'd have said she came back to him because she loved him, missed him. That's what she would have said. And it might have sounded true. She might have been able to make it sound true. Maybe.

Harry read the newspaper article without breathing at all. Without seeming to breathe. Maddie says his lips were wet and his eyes were puffy from crying or anger, or both, and they flickered across the black and white and she saw his mouth part into a pathetic 'O'. Then he looked at her, just very slightly adjusted his gaze, mouth still open, newspaper still raised. She says she thought she saw a spasm of something in the way his eyebrows moved and, unexpectedly, he sat down, maybe looked as though he might be coming at the situation from a different viewpoint.

And she sat down and says she felt the past become the present.

She started sleeping. A lot. Faith did. I stopped losing my temper with her. No point. Anyway, I'd started smoking again. 'Don't smoke,' she said to me. 'Why not?' I said. Her skin was still soft, her flesh. Soft. She'd close her eyes. When I touched her, her eyelids sometimes flickered, like the eyes underneath were awake. And a couple of times she'd shiver as if she'd suddenly fallen into freezing water, or someone had walked over her grave. When she wasn't sleeping, she was telling me she was tired. And the darkness in here was like seeing things through sunglasses worn inside, like light filtered through a lie. And, eventually, she'd lie down, and even though I was telling her what a bitch she was, what a fucking little cunt she was, she lay still. But what struck me most? It was the taste of her, the salt in her sweat, all bitter. It was the goosebumps on her arms, on her neck, on her legs, on the inside of her thighs. That was what struck me most. It was. It was the bitterness, the goosebumps, and the way her eyes flickered as if the eyes were still awake underneath.

When the place started to smell – like cats smell – it wasn't good. I've had to make her sponge off the stains from the mattress. Urine, sweat and whatever. I've made her sponge it all off.

She has to learn.

That's the thing.

I have to make her take responsibility.

When she seemed weak, weakened, I did consider a change of plan, but then I saw the black of her eyes, and it was a near match to something or someone's I've seen before and I knew she had to learn.

Harry hadn't read the article. This is what he says. But he had recognised the girl in the photograph. He'd recognised her straight away. He'd recognised the way she seemed to have everything and nothing in equal parts. He'd recognised the miscalibrated happy arrogance. The ponytail. The blazer with ropes and a lion. When he looked at her face in that photograph, he says he could smell the wet cotton, could taste her breath. He says that Maddie was standing beside him, telling him something about how she hadn't wanted a child, it was all a mistake, how she'd come back to him, Harry, because she'd loved him, missed him, wanted a fresh start.

'You loved me?' he said, and he says his voice grated against the air.

'Yes,' she said, but she wasn't looking at him.

'And did you love the father?'

I sometimes play a CD. 10cc. 'I'm Not in Love'. She used to like it, Faith did. She doesn't seem to now. The notes echo round the walls and seem to add to the perception of depth here. I sometimes put the CD on, and light the candles. Then she knows.

Only once did she ever say, 'Should we really be doing this, Dad?'

But the way I see it is if she can do it with Harry, a stranger, a loser, a taker, a thief, she can do it with me.

'Yes,' I said. 'We should.'

He didn't understand her. I do. She wanted love, real love. Only a father can give that. Only I can do that. It was beautiful. It is beautiful.

And anyway, a woman who disobeys her father is on the wrong side of morality.

Obviously, she'd told me how it all happened. Between her and him. Harry. Said it was all his idea, the hotel. Said he'd told her he wanted to talk to her, just talk. Told her he'd found her fascinating. Afterwards, after she'd told me, she seemed panicked that her father, *her own father*, might not love her any more. So I yielded to her. A little. Had to protect her. Allowed her to touch me. Seemed to absolve her.

That's the way to play this game.

Let them begin to realise how fragile things are. Build them up just enough, just enough, before demolishing everything.

I learned that from her mother.

Yesterday I gave her an apple. Faith. I offered her one. I offered her an apple. 'An apple for the teacher,' I said. It was a kind of joke. I thought I could see her breathing, but I couldn't feel my own, couldn't feel the air in me. I couldn't feel my arm, or the apple in my hand. And when I looked at it, the apple, I thought it was my heart I was giving to her. Thought it was my flesh I was giving to her. I thought it was my blood seeping through my fingers.

But I couldn't be sure.

Maddie drove here. In Harry's car. This is what Harry says. They would have been able to see the hills in the distance – Clent – looking like a couple of heaps of wet rags dumped on the horizon amongst the thin plumes of Black Country smoke. They both say trees lining the dual carriageway were bare-backed, brownish-black, and the fun-fair outside Merry Hill Shopping Centre was in darkness. Harry says it was hard to tell where they were, where the buildings and factories and hills ended and the sky began as a vagueness settled and clung on. And Maddie, he says, her face, was lit copper-green by the light from the dashboard. He says she seemed to know where she was going, her eyes were fixed ahead, it was like she couldn't look at him, like she couldn't stand to look at him. That's what he says.

'Maddie,' he remembers saying as she stopped the car at some traffic lights. 'What are we going to do?'

Maddie didn't answer.

Without moving his head, he says he strained his eyes to the right, slits of eyes she wouldn't be able to see. He says he could see the knuckles of both her hands turn pearly as they gripped the steering wheel. And he says he thought, had a premonition maybe, that they'd be sorry, both of them. Too many crimes in his head. 'I couldn't help myself.' He says the words were quiet when they left him.

And he says Maddie stopped the car. He says she didn't pull over, but stopped in the middle of the road. He says it was a smooth stop, and he saw her knees rise and fall as she braked. On either side of them, on either side of the car, were redundant steel works, chain-link fences and concrete garages. There was something about the place that was still alive. If we had listened, we would have heard something. But Harry wasn't interested in any of that. He says, to him, it was as if nothing was alive, not even him. He says it was as if he'd had the air sucked out of his lungs, as if he'd been punched, hard, as if his heart had been torn out and squeezed and emptied and thrown over that fence into the rubble and dirt of those factories. He says it was as if she couldn't bear to look at him, Maddie. As if she couldn't turn her head to face him. As if she was unable to move.

'I didn't know who she was,' Harry said, and he says he's sure he could just make out Maddie closing her eyes, could just make out the outline of her eyelashes. 'If I'd have known, I wouldn't have touched her.' This was not the way he'd planned it. He hadn't planned any of this. 'She told me she was sixteen, nearly seventeen, for fuck's sake. She looked older.' And Harry would have known he sounded more angry than upset, and he'd have tried to temper it. 'If anyone finds out, I'm finished. Finished.' He says he noticed the windscreen had started to steam up, and the road ahead was disappearing. 'If she's gone missing, it's nothing to do with me. Nothing. I swear.' He says Maddie had her head back against the headrest, he could see her mouth was open. He says her profile looked black against the blue cold, says he wiped his nose on the back of his hand. When Maddie looked at him, when she turned her head and looked at him, he says he couldn't see the way her eyes reflected him. Not any more.

'Don't look at me like that,' he said. 'Don't. I've tried to tell you time after time. I have. I've tried to explain. You just weren't listening to me.'

Harry says he saw her knee lifting again before he could even finish talking to her, and she put the car into gear and drove.

And she drove here.

Small cats share the same instincts as large cats. The same impulses. I read that somewhere. And I'm sure of that now.

It was late when they arrived here, Maddie and Harry. Harry isn't as tall as I'd thought he'd be. Not very tall, close up. He wrings his hands when he talks. You can see all the blood rushing to the thick stubs of his fingertips. See how he squeezes and squeezes, as if he's wringing the information out from inside. I noticed that.

Do we think they actually do remember all this? Do we really believe them? All of this explanation on top of explanation. Harry, with his *I couldn't help myself*s. Why didn't he just say, 'I am the bastard who took your daughter's innocence'? Why didn't Maddie just admit to being a whore who abandoned her responsibilities?

Maddie. She thinks she's been as honest as she can be. She truly does.

She's sexy when she gets upset.

I've hugged her a couple of times. She smells of vinegar, or some kind of acid. And Harry's face – when she rests her head on my shoulder, says she's sorry and all that, Harry's face – it's a picture.

As they talk, explain, I look like I'm listening. Maddie makes these patterns. Patterns with her voice, with her body. I don't know how to say it, how to describe it. I think she believes herself. Believes what she's saying. I think she believes she can talk her way out of it all. Harry's the same. I can't always read what they mean, but I think they've told us all this thinking just uttering the words, letting us hear the words, will put it all right.

They were worried about Faith. So they said.

I said she was sleeping.

Maddie looked sort of relieved. Said something like 'The newspaper article said she was missing.'

She might have looked at Harry then. Just glanced across at him.

'She is,' I said. 'I've disappeared her.'

That was when Maddie stood up, bolt upright. A wave of something – anger, passive anger – rippled across her face. *This isn't what we said*, she seemed to be saying but her thoughts were snagged on thorns. Thorns on the side of a road.

'And him,' I said, 'Cotard. I disappeared him.' And I saw Harry's breath.

Cotard, who might have complicated things even more. Worse than that, he might have taken Maddie from me for good. I know what she's like. I know what she likes. She'd have liked him, with his Bohemian lifestyle and his cameras. He probably would have died on the side of that road anyway. I did him a favour. Funny how things turn out.

'Where is she? Where's Faith? Is she safe?' she said, but it seemed to take a while for the words to come out.

I didn't say, but I'm not even sure what's safe and what isn't, so I just nodded. It seemed like the best thing to do at the time.

I could see Harry eyeing up the cameras in the corner. He's got a fucking nerve. He saw me looking at him. He thinks he can explain it all away.

He can't. Not after what he did with my Faith.

But after a while, I'll admit, I was bored of watching Harry picking away at the skin and the little scabs on the side of his thumb, of feeding off their words, their pain. It was starting to feel like maybe I wasn't there. I had to show them. When I looked, there was a cigarette in my hand. I didn't remember lighting it.

And downstairs, it's burnt, a wettish warmth. I don't keep the best cameras down here. Or the folders. Or pictures. Photographs.

And Faith's here.

There's vomit on the pillow, on the mattress.

Somewhere there's pain, like a trill of minor notes.

I tell Maddie to lend Faith her spirit, if she hasn't already.

I'm using twine on Harry. Maybe I'll do the same on Maddie. Maybe. I don't know yet. And I'm taking photographs, looking at the shots through the viewfinder, then on the camera screen, saving them for later, maybe. I look at them, one by one. I don't even recognise Maddie, or Faith, now. There's a reductive quality about the close-up technique.

Harry's watching me and I hear a sound.

I ask him what he said, but he just looks at me with oversized fear and moves his head once.

I tell him, I say, 'Don't go saying things under your breath and then pretend you haven't said anything.' I tell him it stresses me out. I don't like that. He tells me OK, but he says he doesn't think Faith's breathing, he doesn't think Maddie's breathing, says he's sorry for everything he's done, everything he's caused. Something like that.

I know it smells bad down here. There's a smell of paraffin that I can't get rid of. Maddie noticed it. I know she did. Even in the dark.

There's a pack of cigarettes, half-full, in my pocket. And a lighter.

Shame.

Shame on me.

I go over to the girls, my girls, lying on the mattress. Both of them. I flick bits of food or whatever off the sheet, a bit of apple maybe. Some of it sticks to my fingertip. I can't see exactly what it is in this light, but I put it in my mouth, eat it. I don't taste it. I don't even know if I can taste anything any more, or if I'm really here. I might be dead, run over, beaten, burnt.

I think I am. Dead, that is. I think I am dead, and this is hell. This place, here.

And I can't seem to see clearly any more.

I just can't seem to.

I stop thinking about that. I try to make myself stop thinking about it and I undress Maddie. I think Harry's watching. I can feel him looking. He's in the corner and it's darkest there. Her dress comes off easily and when she's naked, Maddie, when she's naked as sin, I hold her and her skin sticks to me like bindweed, no, like goose-grass, like winter weeds on the side of a road. And when I kiss her, she leaves a taste, like orange peel. I can taste it now, still. And it's like when I kiss her, it's as if everybody I have, everybody and everything I own, are things other people need to have, and it all feels spoilt. All my things have been taken by others. Harry Logue takes my things, Jonathan Cotard, he tried to. I had to – have to – take my things back. Beat the thoughts, burn the thoughts. We can't let people walk all over us in this life. We can't let people keep taking.

I get up off the mattress and I feel Harry stir, but I know he's trying not to. He knows his part in all of this. I pick up a camera, put it down, pick up another, close one eye and look through the viewfinder.

Sometimes, I just take photographs, print them out and put them into folders. I like doing that. It calms me down. Relaxes me.

They're not my cameras though, obviously. I'm not the photographer. I just use them, the cameras. Borrow them, if you like. And now I know I have to clear everything out of my head. Everything. Sometimes I feel like my brain has just rotted away and I need to just clear it all out. Beat it out of me, burn it. Delete it. Delete.

They're not my cameras, but they help me clear out the rot from my head.

So I go ahead and take some photographs, photographs of them all, Faith, Maddie and Harry. I've placed Faith and Maddie closer together. Rearranged their limbs. Really close. Touching. They just bleed into one another. It's like, together, they look like a single figure, oddly contorted.

But the lighting isn't good down here so we can only really make out shadows, ghosts. Even as outlines, though, we can see their skin looks the same. In those photographs, both of them are little girls. Forgiveness might be black and white but victimhood is engrained in their every pore. They should have grown up with more of a sense of danger – both of them – looking behind more often, always imagining the worst thing unfolding. Imagining this. Something like this. They should have.

And then I leave them.

I think I leave them.

They won't try the door but I lock it anyway.

They're quiet now, and I'm looking at the shots of them on the camera screen.

And I feel like I can't feel my heart, beating.

And then I remember, I gave that away.

These are not my cameras. I'm not the photographer. I just use them, the cameras. Borrowed them from someone else who needed to leave my things alone. And now, in my head, I can't think. Sometimes I just feel like my brain has rotted away. I can smell it, rotting away, it smells like paraffin or something, and I need to clear it all out. Delete. They're not my cameras, but they help me clear out the rot from my head.

I check the door is locked a couple more times. Lock us all in. All of us.

There's a camera in my hand. The battery's weak.

One last flick through the photographs.

If I squint, I can just about focus, I can see my girls on the screen. My girls. Mine. I zoom in and see them. They're almost as still in real life as they are on that screen. Almost.

I can't help thinking about the lies. About how it's lies that kill relationships. They do. And I can't help thinking how people have underestimated me. They have. They've underestimated me. And they shouldn't have done that. I didn't deserve that. I trusted people and they let me down. They lied. To me. Madeleine – My Maddie. Faith. Harry. All of them. They lied and they let me down. People shouldn't have underestimated me.

And now I need a cigarette. They make me need a cigarette. I can feel the pack in my pocket. I'll have one in a minute.

But I see my thumb, the side of it, on the edge of the camera, then on the buttons. The thumbnail is dirty. Long, like a claw. I can't think how that could have happened.

I look again and I know what I need to do. I see the button I want. It's red. A red button. I don't know if I feel sad. Maybe I just feel angry. I just know I want it to end. All this. I've had enough of listening, of listening to them, of watching, of working it all out. I have. I'm exhausted by it all. I am. I don't deserve any of this. I look at the button, the red one. I'm thinking bad thoughts and I can hear someone crying or something, and it makes me feel angry again. But they don't know we can hear their thoughts, do they? Suppose they did. Suppose that.

I keep looking at that red button, slide my thumb over it. I press it once, twice.

Wait.

Delete.

Delete all.